Watc[h]

by

Jay Northcote

To Lindsay
love
Jay ♡

Copyright

Cover artist: Garrett Leigh.
Editor: Sue Adams.
Watching and Wanting © 2017 Jay Northcote.

ALL RIGHTS RESERVED

This literary work may not be reproduced or transmitted in any form or by any means, including electronic or photographic reproduction, in whole or in part, without express written permission.
This is a work of fiction and any resemblance to persons, living or dead, or business establishments, events or locales is coincidental.
The Licensed Art Material is being used for illustrative purposes only.
All Rights Are Reserved. No part of this may be used or reproduced in any manner whatsoever without written permission, except in the case of brief quotations embodied in critical articles and reviews.

Warning

This book contains material that is intended for a mature, adult audience. It contains graphic language, explicit sexual content, and adult situations.

Acknowledgements

Thank you to the usual suspects: my editor Sue Adams, for making my words better; my alpha readers Annabelle Jacobs and Lennan Adams for keeping me going and not letting me give up; my beta reader Justyna, and my proof readers: Con Riley, Eli Easton, Jen, Rita, Todd, RJ Scott, and N.R. Walker. And last but never least—thank you to all my readers for supporting me and reminding me on a daily basis why I write.

CHAPTER ONE

Shawn lay on his back and stared unhappily at the ceiling. Cracks were visible where the grey morning light filtered through a gap in the curtains. He sighed, still flooded with shame from the night before.

Beth shifted beside him. The space between their bodies was new; they used to sleep curled around each other. Shawn wasn't sure which of them was pulling away—maybe it was a bit of both.

"Are you awake?" Her voice cut through the early morning silence.

"Yeah." His voice was rough; he wasn't in the mood for a conversation. Talking wasn't going to lead anywhere good.

Last night had been weird.

Their relationship had been shaky for a while. Even before Beth had left for her new fancy job in London—while Shawn stayed in Plymouth stacking shelves—things had slipped into an uncomfortable semi-platonic state. Beth wanted more than he could give, but he didn't want to lose her. What would he be without her? He didn't mean that in a soppy, romantic way, but in an entirely literal way.

His mates had all moved away after graduation, most going on to training or jobs they were excited about. Yet despite getting a decent degree in Business Studies, Shawn had no idea what he wanted to do. Yes, his job in Boots the chemist paid the bills, but it wasn't exactly his life's goal. He should be applying for things, putting himself out there and looking for opportunities. But he was frozen by inertia, unable to work up the energy to try. It all seemed so pointless.

Beth was his anchor in a sea of uncertainty. But for how much longer?

She rolled onto her side and put a hand on Shawn's chest. The tender caress lulled him into a false sense of security before her words stripped it away.

"We need to talk."

Shawn's stomach lurched. *Here it comes. Everyone knows what those four little words mean.* "What's up?" He tried to keep his tone light.

"This isn't working."

Ouch. Straight to the point, then. "Yeah."

There was little point in trying to deny it. She was right. They were friends; they liked each other, but the sexual spark had died out fast, and they both knew it. At first, Shawn had been happy to be in a serious relationship. After two and a half years of working his way through girl after girl, it had been a relief to slow down, stop the exhausting cycle of trying to impress, and focus on building something meaningful. He'd had high hopes, but soon found that without the thrill of the chase, it was difficult to maintain his interest.

Finals had given him the perfect excuse to see less of her, and then, at the end of August, she'd moved away to start her new job. They'd seen each other several weekends since then, taking it in turns to visit, but they'd never managed to rekindle their sex life. It had been perfunctory even on a good night.

"I hoped that maybe if we tried something different, spiced things up a little, it might help. But it didn't work, did it?"

Shawn's face burned with humiliation. "I think that was obvious."

When Beth had presented him with the novelty handcuffs, he'd felt an unexpected thrill of excitement, until he realised that *she* wanted to be the one who was restrained.

He'd tried. He really had. He'd done what she wanted, cuffed her to the bed, teased her, made her come—twice. But all the time he'd been wishing he was the one in her place, imagining how it would feel to be on the receiving end. Then, when she'd finally begged him to fuck her, he hadn't been able to stay hard. He'd done his best, but it had been painfully obvious that he only had a semi. Eventually he'd given up, claiming tiredness and too much booze, even though he'd only had a few beers and she knew it.

Afterwards, they'd lain in uncomfortable silence until they both fell asleep.

Beth's hand still lay on his chest, resting over the thud of his heart. She said, "Maybe if we still lived in the same city, we could try and work things out. But given the distance…."

"Yeah. No. I mean… you're right. We should probably call it quits." Saying the words out loud made Shawn feel a tiny bit better. Agreeing with her made it feel less like being dumped.

"I'm sorry." Her voice was small and soft, like Beth herself.

"It's fine."

It was stupid to mourn a relationship that had died months ago, but Shawn felt like shit anyway, guilty for letting her down, angry with himself for not being able to make it work. But under those emotions lay an undercurrent of fear. Unacknowledged wants and desires swirled, threatening to sweep him away to a place he didn't want to go.

He gently moved her hand from his chest and sat up, scratching his belly. "What time is it?" He answered his own question by picking up his phone. "Nearly eight. What time are you going back?"

"I'm booked on the eleven fifteen."

Shawn didn't mention that was earlier than she usually left. He wondered whether she'd come here this weekend half-expecting to split up with him.

"You hungry?" he asked instead.

"Not very. But I could use some coffee."

"There's a surprise." Shawn managed a chuckle despite the mood of the morning. Full of nervous energy, Beth ran on caffeine and chocolate. He got out of bed and pulled on some sweatpants and socks. It had been chilly yesterday for early October, and the house was never very warm because they tried to keep the heating low to save on bills.

"Some things never change," she said lightly.

"Want it up here or downstairs?"

"I'll come down in a minute."

When it was time for Beth to leave, Shawn insisted on walking with her to the station.

"I'll carry your bag," he said.

"You don't have to do that any more."

"I want to."

It wasn't that Beth couldn't manage her own case, but he needed the finality of seeing her off. He wasn't ready to let go of her on the doorstep, and he didn't want his housemates around for the final goodbye. He would have to tell them what had happened eventually. Jez was a nosey fucker and would soon notice if Beth and Shawn stopped visiting each other, but Shawn wanted to close the chapter with Beth before dealing with telling people it was over.

They walked in silence with the ever-present Plymouth seagulls circling overhead providing a wistful soundtrack. Shawn adjusted Beth's sports bag on his shoulder. The strap dug in but he didn't mind the pain. It gave him a focus for his discomfort, anchoring him in the present. He didn't want to think about the future.

They parted ways at the ticket barrier. It was a weirdly anticlimactic goodbye.

"I'll miss you," she said, her eyes bright with tears. "I still care about you, you know."

"I know. Same here." He pulled her back into his arms for a hug. She clung to him and he wrapped his arms around her. It felt strange offering comfort when she was the one who was leaving him. He briefly wondered how it felt to be hugged by someone bigger and stronger than yourself, or at least someone of a similar size. It must be nice. He remembered his best mate, Mike, trying to hug him sometimes when they got drunk and affectionate on a pub crawl or in a club. Shawn had always pushed him away, uncomfortable with the contact and worried about what people might think.

Beth disentangled herself, interrupting his thoughts. Her eyes were wet now, and she dashed the tears away briskly before giving him a final kiss on the cheek.

"Take care of yourself, Shawn. I hope you find someone who makes you happy. I wasn't the right girl."

"You too. Have a nice life." He meant it to sound like a joke, but it came out sounding bitter, so he clarified. "I mean it. I want you to be happy too."

She smiled. "I know. I have to go or I'm gonna miss my train. I'll see you around on Facebook." She picked up her bag, hefting it onto her shoulder. "Goodbye, Shawn."

"Bye."

She hurried through the barriers, turned the corner onto the platform, and was gone.

Shawn swirled the last dregs of his beer around in the bottom of the bottle. The numbing blanket of alcohol had descended around him, a welcome buffer between him and the world. How many had he drunk tonight? Maybe five… or even six? He'd lost count after the third.

He should probably switch to water and then head to bed; he had an early shift in the morning that meant getting up at seven.

Fuck it. He'd started early and it was only nine o'clock. One more wouldn't hurt.

He drained the bottle, heaved himself out of the armchair, and navigated unsteadily towards the living room door. "Need more beer," he mumbled, then much louder, "*Ouch!*" That was his shin on the coffee table. He stooped to rub it and nearly lost his balance.

"Are you sure about that, Shawny?" Jez asked mildly.

Shawn raised his head and glared at him belligerently.

Jez was all cuddled up with Mac on one of the large sofas. Their hands were laced together on Jez's thigh, and they both looked so fucking smug and happy. The sight of them made something ugly twist in Shawn's stomach.

"Fuck off," he said.

Jez shrugged. "You'll thank me in the morning."

Shawn ignored him and went to the kitchen to get another beer. Jez wasn't his mum, and Shawn could handle his beer. His job wasn't exactly challenging, and it wouldn't be the first time he'd done it with a hangover. He'd done that far too many times since he started working there in July, but whatever.

Back in the living room, he threw himself into his armchair again. The TV was on, showing an old episode of *Prison Break*, but Shawn wasn't paying attention to it. Sunk in a black hole of despondency, he gazed surreptitiously around the room at his housemates instead.

Jude, one of the new guys who'd moved in last month, sat in a corner of one of the sofas doing something on his phone, his dark curly head bending low and the glow of the screen lighting up his angular features. Shawn wondered what he was doing— probably hooking up on Grindr or something.

That twist of discomfort flared in his gut again. He knew he shouldn't care. It was none of his business, but the idea that Jude might be planning some hook-up with some random guy lodged in his consciousness like a stone in a shoe. Maybe it was just because Shawn was single again and would have to get back to hooking up if he wanted any action. The idea of being back on Tinder wasn't as appealing as it should be.

Shawn turned his attention to the other sickeningly happy couple in the room. Ewan wasn't technically one of Shawn's housemates. He lived next door, but he might as well have moved in for the amount of time he spent there with Dev. Ewan had his arm around Dev, and as Shawn watched, he turned his ginger head and murmured something in Dev's ear. Dev turned to look at him and they exchanged a soft smile. Then Dev pressed a kiss to Ewan's lips, which lingered long enough to make Shawn uncomfortable.

Irrational anger bubbled up, spilling out of his mouth before he could hold the words back. "For fuck's sake. Can't you save that for your room?"

Dev pulled away quickly, his cheeks flaming. "Sorry," he muttered.

Ewan glared at Shawn. "What's your problem?"

Shawn shrugged and glared back. "I just don't need to see it, that's all."

"Well, the television's over there, so stop fucking looking at us if you don't like it. It was just a kiss. It's not like we're blowing each other on the sofa or anything. Jesus."

"Ugh. And thank you for *that* mental image." Shawn did a mock shudder.

"Whoa, Shawn. What the hell's wrong with you tonight?"

Jez's voice cut through Shawn's drunken, angry haze, and he realised that all eyes in the room were on him. He caught Jude's gaze, curious and assessing, and flushed at the unwanted attention.

"You should be used to it by now," Jez continued. "You've lived with me and Mac long enough. And I've totally caught you groping Beth on the sofa before. You don't get a free pass for living room shenanigans just because you're the only straight couple in the house since Dani moved out."

That was the spark that ignited Shawn's anger past the point of no return. "Yeah? Well, maybe I'm just tired of being surrounded by all the *gay* in here. I never signed up for this when we moved in together." He stood, sloshing beer out of his nearly full bottle and onto the carpet. "I don't have to like it."

"Feel free to find somewhere else to live, then."

Even Jez, who was rarely moved to anger, sounded pissed now.

"Yeah. Maybe I will." Shawn stormed to the door, careful not to ruin his exit by walking into the coffee table again. "Oh, and for your information? Me and Beth split up today, so we won't be the token straight couple any more."

He slammed the door behind him and stomped up the stairs to his room on the first floor. He slammed that door too, but it didn't make him feel any better. After throwing himself down on the bed, he clutched his pillow and let harsh sobs of fury burst out of him until the red mist receded and shame and guilt crept in to fill the place where his anger had been.

CHAPTER TWO

"What the hell was that about?" Jude asked as the door crashed shut behind Shawn.

He didn't know Shawn that well yet, and this was a side of him he hadn't seen before. Shawn always seemed like a decent enough bloke if you could ignore his toxic masculinity and competitiveness. He was a terrible loser at video games, but apart from that was usually pretty chilled.

"Just ignore him. He's a dick when he's drunk," Jez said.

"Yeah." Mac, his boyfriend, agreed. "But that was worse than he's been in ages. I thought he'd got used to our PDAs by now."

Jez shrugged. "I suppose if he's just split up with Beth, it touched a nerve. Maybe it's more about him feeling unhappy than about us being two guys."

"Didn't sound like it," Ewan said shortly. "He's a homophobic twat. I don't know why you guys put up with him."

"What are we going to do, throw him out?" Jez shrugged. "He pays rent. Maybe he'd be happier if he found somewhere else, though. He's been pretty subdued since Mike moved out. I think he misses him."

"Oh." Ewan raised his eyebrows meaningfully. "You reckon?"

"Not like *that*," Jez said. "Well… I don't think so anyway. They were best mates since our first year. Mike was his wingman."

"You know what they say. It's always the ones deepest in denial who fight the hardest. Maybe he's secretly gay, and that's why he hates having it shoved in his face all the time?"

"That makes sense," Jude agreed. "I was involved with a guy like that at school. He was a total arsehole to me for two years, then finally admitted he wanted to suck my dick."

"Did you let him?" Mac asked.

"Fuck, yes. He was hot."

Jez tried to get the conversation back on track. "Seriously, though, Shawn's always been into girls. Remember what he was like in our first and second year, Mac? He was with a different girl every week."

"Doesn't mean anything," Jude said. "Overcompensation. Classic, isn't it?"

"Yep." Ewan nodded his agreement. "Maybe he has something to prove."

"You just want to believe it because you have a straight-guy kink." Dev nudged Ewan. "I've seen the porn you watch."

Ewan snorted. "Yeah, not even going to try and deny it. But you have to admit it's hot, that whole turning-the-straight-guy thing."

"Oh yeah." Jez patted Mac's thigh. "It's hot as fuck. I turned Mac bi. It was awesome."

Mac snorted. "Yeah, you did, and yeah, it was. But I was never straight, was I? You just made me realise it."

Jude grinned. Jez and Mac were super cute together. "Well, I reckon Ewan could be right about Shawn—he's protesting way too much. He's secretly hankering after cock and doesn't want to admit it."

"You gonna help him work it out?" Ewan smirked. "Might be fun."

"Yeah, if I want my nose broken. I don't think he's ready yet." Jude sighed regretfully. It was a shame, because Shawn was pretty hot. With his short blond hair and blue eyes he reminded Jude of Captain America, and Jude would totally be up for banging him. "Maybe one day." His phone buzzed with a reminder. "Okay, guys. Sorry to leave this hot topic, but duty calls."

"Studying to do?" Jez asked.

"Something like that."

Jude made sure to lock his door behind him when he reached his bedroom on the top floor. Not that it was likely that anyone would barge in, but he wasn't taking any chances. Studying was the last thing on his mind; earning money was his priority this evening.

He set things up quickly, with his laptop open on his desk, angled just right, and the overhead light on so that his clients would be able to see everything clearly. He set his wireless mouse and keyboard on the small table beside his chair in case he needed them—on the left-hand side so his right, his dominant hand, was free.

He checked the time again. 9.28 p.m. *Two minutes till showtime.*

He made sure that lube was within reach on the foot of the bed, along with his favourite dildo in case he was in the mood and the tips racked up high enough.

One minute to go.

Jude kept his T-shirt on but changed his jeans for sweatpants and adjusted his dick, which was already thickening. After six months of this, he'd got himself well trained. Luckily, he was pretty kinky by nature and getting his rocks off for strangers on the Internet turned him on. The money didn't hurt either.

Finally ready, it was time to get started, and with a few clicks of the mouse, he was live.

"Evening, guys. Who's with me tonight?" He drawled, spreading his thighs and lounging back in the chair.

The number of viewers ratcheted up as he watched, hitting double figures within seconds as his regulars logged in for the show.

Immediately the chat messages started pinging in.
Dickseeker21: Hi Tom, you're so hot
Tom was Jude's screen name.
Jojo_69: I'm here and ready 2 cum
Timberxx: Show me ur cock

Jude chuckled. "We'll get to that soon enough. But you know I like to take my time. Don't forget, the more you tip me, the more you'll see."

Timberxx: shirt off?

"When we get to twenty quid." Jude rubbed a lazy palm over the line of his cock, enjoying the tingle and spread of arousal.

He teased them for a while, replying to comments and squeezing his thickening erection through his sweatpants. Occasionally he pushed up the hem of his T-shirt and ran a hand over his stomach. After a couple of minutes, the number of viewers had risen into three figures and the tips edged towards his first goal of twenty pounds.

When the number went high enough, he was inundated with messages.

Shirt off
Show us your chest
Get naked

It was weird to imagine all those nameless, faceless guys out there, with their hands on their dicks waiting to see more of his skin. When he'd first started doing this, Jude had been freaked out by it, intimidated by the idea of an audience, but also ashamed of the fact that it turned him on. He'd quickly adjusted to it and had owned his kink. He wasn't hurting anyone—quite the opposite. He was spreading happiness... and orgasms.

"Okay, okay. It's shirt-off time." Jude stripped out of it slowly enough to make them impatient and then tossed it aside. His erection was obvious now, and he palmed it slowly while he sat back and read the admiring and straightforwardly honest comments.

Hot as fuck
Wanna fuck u
I wd jizz all over u
Love ur chest hair
Fuck I came already

He chuckled at the last one. "You gonna stick with me for round two?"

Pinch ur nipples.

Jude was happy to oblige. He used his free hand to skim over the dark hair on his chest and tease both his nipples until they were hard and sensitive. His dick ached now, the thick fabric of his sweatpants was too much, and he was desperate for more. But he enjoyed the build-up. That was another kink he didn't know he had until he'd started doing this. Edging himself— the delicious anticipation of making himself wait to come—was so good.

Still, it didn't hurt to remind his viewers what they were there for. "Don't forget to tip me, guys. I want to come tonight. But you won't get to see it unless we get up to at least a hundred."

That reminder made the number spike immediately. Jude reckoned they deserved a reward for that.

"Thanks for your generosity. For that, the sweatpants come off."

He stood to slide them down, turning so they got a view of his boxer-clad arse as he eased the waistband past his boner. He gave his bum a slap and a wriggle for all the arse worshippers out there. Jude didn't do a lot of butt stuff. He was more of a top and preferred to just jerk it for the camera. But if the tips went high enough, then he was down for using a toy occasionally. It wasn't a hardship even if it wasn't his favourite thing.

"I'm sticky already," he said as he turned. "Look." He moved closer to the webcam, making sure the wet spot was visible at the head of his dick. "It's going to be hard taking it slow tonight."

U cud cum twice, someone suggested.

"I could. But I think I want to make myself wait. As my regulars know… I'm all about the quality rather than the quantity."

Jude settled back into his chair, legs wide and erection hard and obvious in his boxer briefs.

Damn, he really was horny tonight. He let his mind wander for a little while, teasing his cockhead with his fingertips and tweaking his nipples to keep them hard. An image of Shawn popped into his head, face flushed and angry as he yelled at them earlier. It wasn't a huge stretch of the imagination to think about him flushed for other reasons.

Shawn was totally Jude's type. He had that straight-boy-next-door quality that pushed all Jude's buttons and was ripped as fuck. Jude had seen him in passing on the landing when Shawn was on his way back from the bathroom, wearing only a towel. Shawn obviously spent a lot of time in the gym or was blessed with very good genes, because he was bulky in all the right places and lean in the rest. Jude would happily lick him all over.

"Shit, guys. I'm really fucking horny tonight." He dragged his attention back to the here and now. He had a job to do, and he needed to keep his fans happy.

What r u thinking about? someone asked.

Maybe telling them the truth would work. At least it would give him a focus for the dirty talk.

"I'm thinking about this bloke I know. He's really hot." Jude reached down to squeeze his balls, needing to slow things down a little.

Have u fucked him?
Is he gay?
Does he have a nice dick?
Cut or uncut?

Jude grinned. "No, no, and I don't know. He's definitely not gay. But I wonder if he might be in denial—bi-curious, maybe? I wouldn't mind finding out."

What wd u do to him?

"I'd blow him, and I'd blow his fucking mind."

In among the comments was an increasing number of requests to see his dick.

"We're nearly there, guys. Fifty quid and I'll get it out for you. You know how it works. Believe me, I'm as impatient as you. I can't wait to get it out and jerk it for you."

U cut or uncut? That was obviously a newbie. A few of his regulars immediately jumped in with a barrage of *uncut* replies.

"Yeah, I'm uncut. British boy, you know? So if you want to see me play with my foreskin, hit that tip button, man."

That did the trick, sending his tips zooming past the fifty mark. Jude eased his boxers down below his balls, still sitting. The cool air of the room hit the hot skin of his dick. He tightened his muscles, making his cock flex, and a bead of precome pooled at the tip. It was a shame they probably wouldn't be able to see that. He scooped it off with a finger and licked. "Bet you wish you could suck this for me, huh?"

About twenty replies confirmed this. The admiration turned Jude on even more.

Then one comment caught his attention: *Bet u wish ur straight boy wd suck it for you.*

Fuck. The jerk of Jude's cock was involuntary that time. The image of Shawn's flushed face, lips stretched around Jude's dick as he fed it to him, had Jude gripping himself tightly as he took a shuddering breath.

"Yeah," he said huskily. "Yeah. I really do."

After that it was a battle to make himself last. Jude did all his usual party pieces, tugging on his foreskin and then getting close up to the camera to roll it back and forth over the head. When the tips got to seventy-five, he took his underwear off completely and kneeled backwards on his chair to show off his hole. By the time he'd earned one hundred, he wasn't in the mood to make himself wait any longer.

"No, I'm not going to fuck myself tonight. I want to come. Are you guys ready to come with me? I'm so fucking close now." He leaned back in the chair, thighs spread, stroking himself hard. Tension and need coiled tight, ready to explode.

Do it
I'm ready
Right there with u
So hot

Jude bit his lip, squeezed his eyes shut, and imagined Shawn again—on his knees waiting for Jude to come on his face like the dirty little cum slut Jude wished he was—and that was it.

"Oh fuck, yeah…." Jude groaned as his orgasm ripped through him, his hips lifting as he fucked into his fist. In the moment of pure, blinding pleasure, he forgot about the camera. The world receded, and all that mattered was the perfect physical sensation of climax. Hot splashes of come hit his stomach and chest, and he worked himself through it until he was done, breathless and quivering.

When he came back to earth, he smiled lazily at the messages of approval.

"I'm glad it was good for you. It was fucking awesome for me." He moved his hand so the camera could pick out the semen pooled on the dark hair below his navel. "See you again next time. Midweek show on Wednesday and same time next Sunday. And don't forget—you can follow me on Twitter, Tom underscore Hard underscore On."

Reaching for the mouse, about to end his session, a final message caught his eye.

Get ur straight boy to join u next time. That wd b hot.

Jude chuckled. "Shit, yeah. That would be really hot. But I can't see it happening. Only in my dreams. Okay, night guys. Sleep well. Till next time…." He clicked the mouse and the cam screen went blank.

He sighed. Now the high of the show was over, he slipped abruptly into the strange flatness that usually followed. His room felt too empty. It was only ten-thirty; he'd been pretty fast tonight. Maybe he should head back downstairs for some company? But he wasn't in the mood for hanging around with the happy couples.

It wasn't that Jude was looking for a relationship. He had mates, and had no trouble hooking up. But sometimes after doing a cam show, he got a weird sense of isolation. He'd shared something intimate with a host of strangers on the other side of their computer screens, and for that hour or so, they made him feel special, as if he was important to them.

That was an illusion. He was just a good-looking guy with a decent dick who knew how to work it for the camera. If he stopped doing his show, nobody would miss him. They'd find another pretty guy to jerk off to instead.

CHAPTER THREE

On Monday, Shawn made it through his shift at Boots with the help of energy drinks and paracetamol. His head ached from the beer the night before. That was understandable.

The ache in his chest was harder to explain.

At least he wasn't on the tills today. Instead he was stacking things onto the shelves, taking some comfort in the mindless, methodical work.

Why am I such a dick after alcohol?

He was ashamed of his outburst the night before. Jez and Mac were his friends, and although he didn't know Ewan and Dev very well, that was no excuse for what he'd said.

When Jez and Mac had first come out—well, not so much "come out" as been forced out of the closet when Shawn walked in on them in bed together— Shawn had been shocked to his very core.

He'd had no idea that Jez and Mac were gay. No, not gay—they were bi. Not that you'd know it since they were monogamous and sickeningly in love with each other. But Shawn had learned a lot in the last year or so, and he understood now that Jez and Mac would always be bi even if they never fucked another woman in their lives.

He'd got used to their relationship, accepted it, and tried not to be a dick about it. But deep down it still made him uncomfortable seeing two guys together, and the discomfort made him guilty, and the guilt made him angry. Somehow his break-up with Beth had been the last straw.

He sighed, glaring at the can of deodorant in his hand as though it had personally offended him. When he got home tonight, he'd apologise. He owed them that.

Because he was a masochist, Shawn went running as soon as he got home from work. By the time he got back to the house again and had showered and changed, it was just after six and all five of his housemates were battling for space in the large shared kitchen.

Even Ben was there, the quiet mature student who'd moved in at the same time as Jude. When he wasn't cooking or eating, he spent most of his time in his room, so they barely saw him.

As Shawn came in, Jez and Mac looked up and nodded in greeting. But even Jez's usually friendly face was guarded and his nod was curt.

Shawn couldn't blame him. Bracing himself, he cleared his throat.

"Um. About last night…."

All heads turned to him. Jez, Mac, Jude, and Dev had their eyebrows raised expectantly.

Ben frowned. "What?"

"You weren't there, mate," Jude said.

Ben shrugged and went back to spreading something on toast, but it was obvious he was still listening.

Shawn's cheeks heated with shame as he remembered his childish outburst. "I was a dick and totally out of line, and I'm sorry. You have just as much right as I do to kiss and cuddle… or whatever, in public. I was just being an arsehole because I was drunk, and because of splitting up with Beth. I had a shitty weekend, but I shouldn't have taken it out on you." He addressed Dev directly. "Can you pass my apology on to Ewan, please?"

"Sure." Dev nodded.

Shawn waited, palms sweating and heart pounding as he scanned Jez's and Mac's faces for a reaction, but they remained serious.

"You were a *total* dick," Jez finally said, "but that was a pretty decent apology. So I'll take it. Just don't do it again, you twat."

He came over to Shawn and punched him playfully in the arm, almost hard enough to hurt.

Shawn didn't flinch. He deserved it. "Thanks, man," he said gruffly. He glanced at Mac, then Dev. "We good now?"

"Sure." Mac shrugged.

Dev gave a small smile. "Yeah."

Only then did Shawn shift his gaze to Jude, who was watching the scene unfold, his face impassive. Shawn didn't feel that he needed to apologise to Jude; he hadn't had a go at him directly. But Jude was gay, and Shawn's homophobic comments had probably pissed him off too. "Sorry," he muttered.

Jude held his gaze, his brown eyes hard to read. A muscle ticked under the dark stubble on his jaw. "No worries. We all say stupid things when we're drunk. Forget about it."

Relief and gratitude swept through Shawn. He wasn't sure he deserved such casual forgiveness; he wasn't going to forgive himself so easily. Fleetingly he wondered why Jude's good opinion of him mattered so much, but then he pushed the thought away.

He broke the tension, rubbing his hands together. "Okay, well, I'm starving. Gonna see what I've got in the fridge."

They all went back to what they were doing and Shawn relaxed, his apology over with and accepted.

A couple of days later, Shawn was still doing his best to be a better housemate and friend. So after he'd finished his dinner—late because he hadn't left work till six and had then been running again—he washed up lots of pots in the kitchen that other people had used and tidied up some things left lying around in the living room.

"Is this either of yours?" He held up a hoodie that was slung over the back of a chair.

Jez and Mac, who were on the sofa watching TV, both glanced his way.

"Nope," Mac said.

"I think it's Jude's."

Being helpful, Shawn decided to take it up for him.

He passed his own bedroom on the middle floor and went up the second flight of stairs to where Dev's and Jude's rooms were. Jude's door was shut, so Shawn tapped lightly on it. There was no reply, so assuming Jude was out, he turned the handle and pushed. The door opened quietly.

It took a moment for his brain to register the information from his eyes.

Jude wasn't out.

Jude was definitely *in*.

He was sitting in a chair with his back to the door, shirtless, dick out and jerking off in front of... fuck, was that Skype? Maybe he had a long-distance boyfriend Shawn didn't know about.

But the screen didn't look like Skype; there was a distinctive logo that even from the door, Shawn could see read "Boyz on Cam." And—*Oh fuck*. The guy on the screen looked remarkably like Jude himself. Surely he couldn't be...?

"Shit, sorry, sorry!" Shawn blurted out.

"What the fuck?" Jude wheeled around, simultaneously managing to whip his sweatpants up and slam the laptop shut. "Oh my God, haven't you heard of knocking?"

"I did knock," Shawn said helplessly, trying not to stare at the bulge in Jude's trousers. *Eyes up. Jesus Christ, don't make this any worse than it already is.* "You didn't answer."

"I didn't fucking hear you. But you just barged in anyway." Jude covered the tent in his sweatpants with his hand.

His face was flushed. It was hard for Shawn to tell how much was embarrassment and how much was anger. "You should have locked it," he said unhelpfully, then mentally kicked himself for his lack of filter. *Bit late to point that out now.*

"I thought I had!"

"I'm sorry," Shawn said again. "I didn't... I mean...." Sensible words eluded him. There was no script for this. "I found this. It's yours. I'll go now." He threw the hoodie at Jude, turned, and fled, shutting the door firmly behind him.

Back in his own room, Shawn paced back and forth.

"Fuck, fuck, *fuck!*" He scrubbed his hands through his hair, stopped pacing, and glared at his laptop where it lay on his desk, a threatening presence.

No. I can't.

He threw himself down on the bed and stared at the ceiling.

But what if he was wrong? Maybe he'd misinterpreted what he saw? Maybe Jude was just watching another guy on camera who happened to look a bit like him? Shawn tried to tell himself that it was none of his business anyway, but he needed to know.

He got up and locked his door—learning from Jude's mistake there—then sat at his desk and opened his laptop carefully, as if it was an unexploded bomb he had to defuse. He pulled up his web browser and typed in the words burned onto his brain: Boyz on Cam.

After an 18+ warning, the site loaded quickly and Shawn half covered his face with a hand, as though peeking through his fingers could make this better. He scrolled past a few photos of half-naked guys with nice abs and inviting smiles, but none of them was Jude.

Then he noticed a link at the top reading "Live Shows."

Mouth dry and heart racing, he clicked on it. He didn't think it was possible for his heart to beat any faster, but when he saw Jude's face grinning suggestively at him from a thumbnail image, he seriously wondered if it was possible to have a heart attack at the age of twenty-one.

He knew he shouldn't look, didn't even know why he wanted to go any further. He'd confirmed his suspicions, and that was all he needed to know. Yet, with a shaking hand, he clicked on the link anyway.

Immediately, Jude's voice came out of his speakers, tinny but unmistakable. "Anyway, let's get back to business, guys. Sorry about the interruption. I thought I'd locked my door, but obviously not. I guess my housemate will be more careful in future, huh?"

Jude was sprawled in his chair again, still wearing sweatpants, rubbing at his soft bulge, teasing it back to hardness. Shawn's interruption had obviously put him off his stride.

Then Jude chuckled. "No, he's straight."

Confused for a moment, Shawn wondered who he was talking to. Intent on watching Jude, he hadn't noticed the chat box on the side of the screen. He glanced at it and saw the barrage of messages.

Wanna see ur cock again
Hurry up
Is ur housemate gay?

Then another message popped up as Shawn watched.

Is he hot?
Would you do him?

"Yeah, he's hot as fuck. He's the one I was telling you guys about last time, remember? And yes, I totally would if I thought there was any chance he'd let me."

Shawn gaped at the screen, an uncomfortable blend of emotions swirling in his stomach. *What the hell?* Jude thought he was hot, and he'd been telling his customers—clients, whatever they were—about *him* while he was jerking off on camera? He wasn't sure whether to be horrified or flattered. Maybe a bit of both?

But before he had time to work out his feelings, he was distracted because Jude got his cock out again and started stroking it slowly and obviously.

This was so wrong. So, so wrong on so many levels of wrongness. And yet Shawn couldn't tear his eyes away. He'd never seen another guy jerk off before; he'd never wanted to. But something about the slide of Jude's hand and the sight of the head popping out of his fist on every stroke was mesmerising.

Without conscious thought or guidance, Shawn's hand found its way to his dick. He squeezed himself through his sweatpants, shocked to find that he was half-hard.

Maybe it was normal to be turned on by this? Watching another guy wanking was making Shawn think about wanking; that must be it. Shawn liked wanking—who didn't? And once the idea was in his head, it seemed logical that he would want to jerk off too.

He shook his head. It wasn't that he thought Jude was hot. Because Shawn wasn't into guys. He liked girls. He liked tits and pussy, and just because it hadn't worked out with Beth, it didn't change that. Shawn had had good sex with girls, *lots* of good sex, and he'd never been interested in a guy before.

Before? Where the fuck had that come from? Shawn locked it down tight. This wasn't interest.

But he had his hand in his boxers now and was moving it in time with Jude's, as his gaze roved over Jude's body.

Jude was hot. Shawn could appreciate that in a totally objective way. But it was more that he admired him than fancied him. He didn't want to *bang* Jude, but he wouldn't mind looking like him. He had always wanted more body hair. It looked so much more masculine than his own mostly smooth chest. What little body hair he had was sandy blond, so it hardly showed unless it caught the light. Jude's chest and belly had a generous sprinkle of dark hair, with a thick line leading down to his cock.

Shawn stared at Jude's cock and heavy balls, and he let his brain stop. Thinking was too difficult when all he wanted to do was watch and jerk himself off in tandem with Jude. There would be plenty of time for a sexual identity crisis later.

Pacing himself was an exercise in endurance, but it became a matter of weird pride that he shouldn't come until Jude did. Guys in the chat window came and went—literally, but a few seemed to enjoy making themselves wait till the grand finale.

Usually when Shawn jerked off, he didn't take long. It was all about releasing tension and not taking pleasure in the act itself, but this was different. Making himself wait made the pleasure build until he reached a point where orgasm was just a few firm strokes away and the anticipation was a desperate, wonderful knife-edge.

Jude was waiting for his tips to reach a certain point before he gave his viewers what they wanted. It was a good system. If Shawn was a member, he'd have paid any amount of money to see him come so that he could finally join him.

"Thanks for your generosity, guys," Jude said. The strain was showing in his voice now, a thread of need that made Shawn's balls ache in sympathy. "I'll give you a little extra treat today as we've made it over a hundred and fifty. Who's ready to come?"

A flood of replies indicated that there were a lot of people out there waiting for that.

In preparation, Shawn pushed his sweatpants and boxers down around his ankles and spread his thighs wide. He cupped his balls with one hand, feeling how high and tight they were. He gripped his cock with the other, not even moving his hand yet, too close to risk it.

On-screen, Jude moved and reached for something, and Shawn's eyes flew wide as he realised what Jude had picked up—a black dildo, average-sized with a flared base and handle. Jude coated it with lube and then leaned back in the chair, bending his legs and putting his heels on the seat by his arse.

Holy shit!

Shawn stared at Jude's hole. This made him feel dirtier than anything else had so far. The knowledge that Jude was doing this on the floor above, right now, and had no idea Shawn was watching him felt like a violation. But Jude was doing it on camera for anyone to see. Shawn wasn't doing anything wrong and he couldn't look away.

He kept his eyes fixed on the screen as Jude eased the dildo into himself. Shawn's own arse muscles squeezed as Jude gave a little grunt when it slid home.

Shawn slid the hand on his balls a little lower, pressing curious fingertips against his hole. He'd never touched himself there except to wash, never let his hand linger. He'd done anal with girls, but never let any of them use their fingers or mouth on him there. He'd shut them down immediately if they'd tried—"I'm not into that." But the truth was, he had no idea if he'd be into it. He'd never dared try because he associated it with being gay, and he was straight— or so he'd always told himself.

Surprisingly, it felt good. The skin was sensitive and the touch of his fingers sent sparks of sensation to his balls and dick. He started to stroke his cock again and watched as Jude began to fuck himself with slow, careful strokes of the dildo.

"Fuck," Jude gritted out. "That feels so good. It's hitting my prostate just right. Not gonna take long. Are you imagining this is your cock in me? Fucking me? You gonna fuck me harder?"

Shawn couldn't tear his gaze away to check the chat box and see whether anyone was replying. He wanted to forget about the other watchers, anyway. He wanted to pretend that Jude was talking to him, and him alone.

"Yeah," he muttered. "Fuck yeah."

"Or are you fucking yourself with your fingers or a dildo and wishing it was my cock you were sitting on? Your arse feels so good, so tight. You're gonna make me come...."

Shawn's brain imploded. That image made fireworks go off in his head and his balls. He pressed two fingers against his hole, gasping as his whole body tensed and released. Thick strings of come spilled from his cock as he watched Jude on-screen, joining him in an orgasm that seemed to go on and on until they were both shaking and panting.

"Fuck," Jude said weakly, "that was a good one. I hope it was good for you too." He held his hand up to the camera, a web of come linking his fingers. "So much jizz tonight. I'll see you next time, guys. Sunday night, and don't forget to check my profile and follow me on social media if that's your thing. Tell your buddies where to find me. Sweet dreams."

Jude loomed close to the camera, blew it a kiss, and then the feed went blank.

Alone in the silence of his room, Shawn came back from the heady fantasy to the cold reality of his situation. Seated in his desk chair, pants around his ankles, there was no way he could get away from the fact that he'd just masturbated over a video of his housemate.

His gay, male housemate.

And he'd come harder than he'd ever come in his life.

Fuck.

Shawn scrubbed himself clean in his second shower of the evening as though he could wash away the memory of what he'd done. His perception of himself had skewed, like a warped looking glass showing a reflection he didn't recognise.

One wank over a dude doesn't make me gay.

He glared at himself in the fogged bathroom mirror. He didn't *look* any different. The world didn't need to know.

Later that night, in bed, he pulled up Tumblr on his phone and looked through the posts he'd saved by liking them. All beautiful women, barely a man in sight. He rarely saved images with guys in them. He scrolled through the pictures, admiring soft curves, feminine nipples, vaginas. Despite his earlier orgasm, his cock responded. He couldn't be bothered to jerk off again, but it was good to know that part of him hadn't changed.

I still like girls.
But maybe I like guys too?

All the evidence from tonight seemed to point to that, but Shawn wasn't sure what to do with the information. How could he not have realised before?

The answer was obvious…

Because you never let yourself.

Growing up, Shawn had been one of those boys who went through puberty late. Still embarrassingly small and skinny at fourteen, he'd been horribly self-conscious about his high voice and lack of height compared to his peers. He'd been teased—because some kids are stupid like that—but the words hurt.

Girly, sissy, gay, wimp.

When the testosterone fairy finally visited him and he had a growth spurt, Shawn started going to the gym, and he'd worked his body hard to make it change faster. He'd become aggressively competitive, lifting heavier weights and training harder than the other guys he knew. And when his newfound muscles and confidence started to earn him the attention of girls, Shawn had thrown himself into dating, proving himself that way too.

When he left school, he launched himself into the social scene at university with the same attitude and worked his way through a string of girls until he settled down with Beth for while. And all that time, if he ever found himself looking at another guy in the changing rooms or in the weight room at the gym, he'd convinced himself it was envy, not admiration.

Denial was a powerful thing.

Sighing, Shawn put his phone aside. He turned his lamp off and lay in the darkness. His mind whirled with possibilities that terrified him, but there was a thread of excitement intertwined with the fear.

So what if he was bi? Jez and Mac had come out and the world hadn't ended. Maybe it was time he finally let himself explore the things he'd been hiding from for so long. He didn't have to tell anyone else about it unless he wanted to.

CHAPTER FOUR

Jude hated that he felt ashamed.

He'd never felt ashamed of what he did before. Maybe because he'd grown up with such a liberal mother, he had always been completely accepting of his sexuality and choices. She had been a single mum and a telephone sex worker to make ends meet. She'd tried to keep it a secret from Jude, but one day, when he was fifteen, he'd come home from school early and caught her working. She'd been doing the ironing with her back to the door, wearing a headset. She hadn't heard Jude come in, but he'd heard every shockingly filthy word coming out of her mouth.

She'd explained to him that it was a job, it paid well, and how else did he think she could afford to buy him decent trainers and pay for his phone contract?

"Anyway." She shrugged. "It's not hurting anyone, nobody's being exploited, and I'm actually making people very happy."

When Jude thought about it, he had to agree with her, and he felt exactly the same about his cam work now—or at least he had done.

Jude waited until the following night to get Shawn alone.

When Shawn went up to his room after dinner, Jude left it a little while, sitting on the sofa and half-watching TV while he worked up the courage to go and face him.

He wasn't entirely sure what Shawn had seen, but he wasn't taking any chances. Jude would rather be clear about what he was doing and see Shawn's reaction for himself. He hadn't told his housemates what he did to earn money, not because he was ashamed of it, but because he didn't think it was their business. Plus, some people could be judgemental twats.

Speaking of judgemental twats, of all his housemates, it was fucking typical that it was Shawn who'd walked in on him, especially after the fuss he'd caused the other day over Dev and Ewan kissing.

Sighing, he got up. *Right, better get this conversation over with.*

Upstairs, Jude knocked loudly on Shawn's door and waited for a response before he entered, opening the door slowly as if to prove a point.

Shawn was sitting on his bed with his laptop, and he looked up as Jude entered. Jude wasn't sure what reaction to expect, but the slightly hunted look that crossed Shawn's features confused him. He forged on.

"Hey," he said confidently, determined to be in control of the situation. "So, I wanted to talk to you about yesterday."

"Uh… yeah." Shawn's face turned bright red and his gaze skittered around the sides of Jude, as though he couldn't bring himself to look directly at him. "I'm so sorry. Again. For bursting in like that."

"Whatever." Jude waved his hands. "Too late for that now. I don't know what you think you saw, but I wanted to be clear about it. I do a sex cam show, and that's what I was doing when you walked in. For money," he added, in case that wasn't clear.

"Oh, right. I kind of figured when I saw…." Shawn gestured vaguely at his laptop, or maybe his crotch because it was covering it—Jude stifled a grin. "Yeah. Okay."

Shawn was still blushing and clearly uncomfortable.

Jude stood awkwardly by the bed with his hands in his pockets. "Look. I'm not ashamed of it. I enjoy it, actually, and I make good money. But I prefer people not to know about it because they can be weird about stuff. I don't want people judging me—like you're obviously doing now."

"I'm not!" Shawn protested. "Seriously. Whatever, man. I won't tell anyone. I'm interested, actually."

"Interested?" Jude arched an eyebrow. "Want me to send you a link?"

Shawn made a weird noise, something between a cough and a splutter, and his blush deepened. "I didn't mean interested like *that*," he finally managed in a hoarse voice. "Just… you know. How did you get into it? And how much do you earn and stuff? It's a bit different to working part-time in a bar or a shop."

Jude studied Shawn and decided the enquiry was genuine. "I met a guy on Twitter who did it, and asked him how to get started. I usually earn at least a hundred quid a show. I do two shows a week, so it adds up."

"Wow. That's cool. Beats the eight quid an hour I get at Boots anyway. And you don't have to wear a stupid uniform."

"Nope." Jude grinned. "In fact, clothing is optional."

Shawn snorted then. "Yeah, so I noticed."

Jude laughed, and Shawn laughed too, and Jude was suddenly sure that it wasn't going to be a problem. "Okay, man. I'll leave you in peace. But thanks for saying you'll keep it to yourself. I prefer it that way."

Even after their conversation, Jude felt a little uncomfortable around Shawn for the rest of the week.

Admitting his attraction and letting himself think about Shawn while jerking off on camera had sparked a crush that was stronger than he was happy with. And then having Shawn walk in on him like that... in a weird way it turned him on to know that Shawn had seen him with his dick out. His exhibitionist streak liked that way too much.

Jude jerked off on Friday night with his door unlocked, half hoping that Shawn would barge in again. Of course he wouldn't, he'd learned his lesson. But Jude let himself imagine it was possible. He turned his chair to face the door, and as he stroked himself to climax, he thought about Shawn walking in. He pictured his confused, flushed face, the dawning realisation as he saw what Jude was doing. He imagined looking down and seeing Shawn getting hard despite himself, turned on by watching Jude, seeing Jude's cock. It didn't take long for him to come with those images in his head.

It would have been easier to ignore his crush if Shawn had been a twat again. But since his outburst the weekend before, Shawn had been trying really hard to be nice. He was making the effort to hang out with the rest of them more, maybe because he was lonely now he didn't have Beth to visit or Skype with.

On Sunday morning, Jude was up and drinking a banana smoothie before heading out to the university gym.

Shawn came in, also dressed in workout clothes. He looked good. His legs still had a light tan from the summer, and Jude liked the way the blond hairs glinted when they caught the light. They looked soft, and he wondered how they'd feel under his hands. He dragged his gaze up, past Shawn's broad chest—showcased by a short-sleeved compression shirt—to his face.

"Morning." Jude leaned back against the kitchen counter.

"Hi," Shawn said gruffly.

He looked a little pink; had he already been out running? He wasn't sweating, so probably not. Shawn ducked away from Jude's gaze and went to the fridge to get some orange juice.

"You heading to the gym?" Jude asked.

"Nah. I'm not a member any more. Not a student, remember."

"But it's open to the public too."

"Yeah?" Shawn scratched the back of his neck. His bicep bulged distractingly. "I didn't know that."

"Yeah. I think it might cost a bit more than the student rate, but you can definitely join—or pay as you go."

"Huh." Shawn glanced out of the window. The sky was dark grey and rain splattered against the glass, caught on a gust of wind. "That's appealing on a day like today."

"Yeah, it is. Why don't you come with me? You can pay for a one-off session and see if you reckon it's worth forking out for membership."

Jude usually worked out alone. It might be nice to have company, and Shawn would definitely improve the view—not that there was a shortage of fit blokes in the uni gym. It kinda went with the territory.

Shawn frowned and the flush was back. Maybe, after the accidental free show he'd got the other day, he felt as weird around Jude as Jude did around him. But that was all the more reason to get past this.

Perhaps Shawn reached the same conclusion, because he finally said, "Yeah, okay, seems like a good idea. Running any distance in this weather isn't appealing, and there's a limit to what I can do with dumbbells in my room. You know what they say, use it or lose it." He flexed his arms and gave Jude his first genuine grin of the morning.

Jude smiled back. "Cool."

The sports centre was only a short jog away, so they ran there as a warm-up. Even that short distance had Jude's shirt wet and clinging to him by the time they arrived; he wished he'd worn something tighter. He showed his membership card at the desk and waited for Shawn while he paid the one-off fee.

"More cardio first? Or weights?" Jude asked after they put their keys and Shawn's wallet in a locker.

"I always do weights first. You get better results that way."

"Yeah? Okay, cool."

They hit the free weights, and Jude was happy to let Shawn take the lead. He seemed to know what he was doing, and Jude was no expert. He'd always kept fit but had never taken weight training quite as seriously as Shawn obviously did. They ended up doing a circuit that targeted more muscles than Jude usually hit in one session, and he was soon feeling it.

"This is gonna hurt tomorrow, man," he complained after a particularly brutal set of lateral raises with a heavier weight than he normally used.

"But it's so good for your delts." Shawn took the weights Jude offered. "Come on, one more set each."

Shawn moved to face the mirror, but Jude could still see his face in the reflection.

"Sadist. It's a good thing you're pretty."

Shawn's gaze flickered to him and a nervous expression crossed his features before he schooled them into impassivity again. He grunted as he raised the weights out to the side, muscles straining, teeth gritted.

"Oh, relax." Jude folded his arms and kept his eyes up, although the temptation to admire Shawn's arse was strong. "You're straight. I get it. Does that mean you can't take a compliment from a gay guy?"

"I s'pose not," Shawn panted out between reps.

"Well, good. Because you're easy on the eye. But I'm pretty sure you know that anyway." Jude winked at him and turned away to stretch his hamstrings, which were stiffening up after some dead lifts they'd done earlier.

When they were finally done, they jogged back to the house. Well, Shawn jogged; Jude felt like he was limping.

"I think you broke me, dude," he panted as he tried to keep pace with Shawn.

"Take it easy for the rest of the day. It'll hurt even more tomorrow, but you'll live."

"I have to work later. Sunday's one of my regular show days." Fuck it if it made Shawn uncomfortable. He knew what Jude did for cash, and Jude wasn't going to avoid mentioning his job now it was out in the open between them.

Shawn snorted. "Jerking off isn't exactly running a marathon. I'm sure you'll cope."

"You'd be surprised. A five-minute fap, yeah, that doesn't take much effort. But my shows sometimes last an hour and a half or even more. That can be tiring, depending on what I do for the camera. I have to work hard to earn those extra tips."

"I don't want to know," Shawn said gruffly.

They'd reached the house now. Jude stretched out his quads while Shawn got out his door keys.

Jude took pity on him and changed the subject. "So, do you reckon you'll join the gym again? It seemed like it was your spiritual home, so you must miss it." He followed him down the hallway to the kitchen.

Shawn went straight for the fridge and started drinking milk out of the carton. His throat bobbed enticingly, and when he was done, there was a distracting drop of milk at the corner of his mouth. He wiped it away with the back of his hand. "Yeah, maybe? I'm not sure. I don't earn much, and I'm still paying off an overdraft."

"That sucks." Jude remembered how tight money had been in his first year before he'd started his cam work.

"I might be able to afford it after Christmas, especially if I can do some overtime." Shawn put the carton back in the fridge. "Right, I'm going to have a shower—as long as one of the bathrooms is free."

"Same. But I'll go after you if the other one's occupied." There were two bathrooms, one on each of the floors that had bedrooms.

Shawn went upstairs first, and Jude followed. It was impossible not to admire Shawn's arse from this angle. Muscular and strong, he had a perfect bubble butt. Jude bet it would look fucking amazing without clothes covering it. He tilted his head and sighed appreciatively. Shame he'd never get a chance to bite it.

That evening, Jude came down to find Shawn and Ben in the kitchen. Shawn stood at the hob, and Ben was dishing up a plate of chips, spaghetti hoops, and what looked like veggie sausages.

Jude wrinkled his nose. Veggie sausages were just *wrong*. He turned to the fridge and opened it to see what he had that looked edible.

"Fuck. I really should have gone shopping today," he muttered.

There was a lump of cheese and some milk and margarine that belonged to him, but not much else.

Jude's cupboard was pretty bare too. Rice, pasta, a couple of potatoes that were starting to sprout, and a can of baked beans. "Jacket potato, beans and cheese it is, then. Again." He'd had the same thing yesterday. He really needed to buy some vegetables.

"You can have some of this if you want," Shawn said without turning. He was busy stirring some delicious-smelling thing. "You're not veggie, are you?"

"God no. I love meat."

Shawn chuckled. "You just can't help yourself, can you?"

"Fuck." A flush heated Jude's cheeks as he realised what he'd just said, but he laughed too. "I wasn't even trying, honestly. I just open my mouth and things happen. It's a special skill."

Shawn glanced sidelong at him, eyebrows raised and lips twisted in a smirk.

"Okay, that one was deliberate." Jude grinned, unapologetic.

"Do you want some of this or not? It's beef mince and onions. I'm having it with mash, peas, and carrots."

"If you're sure. Have you got enough?"

"Yeah, I always cook extra and freeze some for the nights I work late. But you can have it. You need to keep your strength up—after killing it at the gym this morning."

Shawn had hastily added the last part, and Jude guessed where his mind had gone. "Cheers, mate. I'll return the favour soon, once I've been shopping."

"Okay, cool."

"Need any help?"

"Nah, it's nearly done. But you could get some plates and cutlery ready."

They ate in the living room at the large table by the window. Ben was there too with his food. Jez and Mac were lounging on the sofa with an open takeaway pizza box on the table in front of them, slices of pizza in their hands. Normally Jude would have looked at it enviously, but with the meal Shawn had made in front of him, he was impervious to the lure of pizza.

"This is great, thank you," he said after his first mouthful. It really was; he wasn't just being polite. "I didn't know you could cook."

"I have hidden depths." Shawn gave a smug smile.

After they'd eaten, Jude and Shawn hung around in the living room for a while. Ben had gone back to his room, and Jez talked the rest into a game of *Mario Kart*.

"Is Shawn allowed to play again?" Mac asked. "I thought he was on a lifetime ban after last time."

Jude snorted. "What happened?"

"Fuck you!" Shawn's voice rose in outrage. "I didn't meant to throw the controller. I just forgot I didn't have the wrist strap on."

"Yeah, but if you hadn't had a tantrum over losing, it wouldn't have happened, would it? Shit happens, dude."

That was Jez, looking thoroughly amused.

Shawn's expression was dangerously close to a pout. "Yeah, but if you two hadn't ganged up on me and kept pushing me off the track on Rainbow Road, I *wouldn't* have lost."

It shouldn't have looked cute, but it sort of did. "Aw, baby, were the other kids mean to you?" Jude teased.

Shawn glared at him but then shook away his irritation. "Whatever, fuckers. Are we playing or not?"

They played, and Shawn did his best to be a graceful loser when Jez and Mac kept winning. Jude was too amused by Shawn's rising irritation to care that he came last in nearly every race.

After Jez won again and Shawn came third as usual, Jude's phone buzzed with the reminder he'd set up a while ago to alert him in time for his shows.

"Okay, I'm done," he said. "I'll leave you guys to it."

"Can't take the heat?" Mac grinned.

"Yeah, yeah. You and Jez clearly spend way too much time playing that game." Jude put his controller down on the coffee table and stood, stretching. "I've got better things to do."

"Are you up for another round, Shawn?" Jez asked.

"Nah, not tonight. I've, uh, got stuff to do too." Something in his tone made Jude glance his way. But Shawn had his eyes down, untangling the wrist strap.

"Okay, thanks for the game, guys," Jude said, then added, "and thanks for dinner, Shawn. I owe you one."

Shawn looked up then. "No worries." He smiled, and Jude held his gaze for a moment. His stomach did a little flip. Smiling was a really good look on Shawn.

"Bye, then." Jude tore himself away, silently cursing himself for his inability to control his crush.

Still, at least it would give him something to think about during his show tonight.

CHAPTER FIVE

Shawn's anticipation had been building with every hour that passed.

Even though he'd spent most of the day trying to convince himself that he wasn't going to watch Jude's show that evening, all along he'd known he was fighting a losing battle with his conscience.

He told himself it was experimental, all part of his journey of sexual self-discovery that he'd embarked on unintentionally. That was a shitty excuse too, though, because it wasn't like Jude's show was the only porn on the Internet. If he wanted, Shawn could find a thousand other cam boys or porn clips to watch in order to satisfy his bi-curiosity—and at some point, maybe he would. But the urge to watch Jude again was like the pull of the moon on the sea— powerful and irresistible.

Shawn settled on his bed with his laptop, his door locked, and a box of tissues handy. Actually, he didn't even feel guilty any more. Horny as fuck already, he resigned himself to being a creeper, and smiled.

Jude would never need to know.

An hour and a half and two pretty awesome orgasms later, Shawn was regretting his life choices again. Jude was still going, pacing himself and waiting for his tips to rise before he came for his invisible audience.

Shawn hadn't been able to hold out tonight; he hadn't wanted to. He'd raced towards his first orgasm but took more time with the second. Tired and sated, he still couldn't tear himself away. Instead he was watching Jude, amused by the way he interacted with the commenters. It was impressive how he played his crowd and responded to as many of them as he could. His easy smiles and humour were so appealing. No wonder he was popular.

Did ur mate ever say anything about catching u?

The question caught Shawn's attention.

"Oh yeah, but it was no big deal," Jude said. "He was chilled about it."

Even though nobody in the chat room knew he was eavesdropping, Shawn's skin prickled. He felt as though a hundred pairs of eyes were on him.

Bet he's thinking about ur dick.

Jude laughed. "I wish. He's straight, remember?"

Shawn stiffened. Did Jude *really* wish that?

"I went to the gym with him this morning, though," Jude added, a dreamy quality to his voice. "Man… he's built. Great biceps, and his thighs… fuck." His hand moved faster on his dick. "He has *seriously* good thighs."

Shawn's whole body flushed at the compliment. It was weird to know that Jude thought of him like that.

Or did he, really? Maybe it was all just an act for the camera, more dirty talk.

Get him to do a show with u? one commenter suggested.

Another user added, *We'd tip extra for that.*

The chat box went crazy.

Hell yes
Yeah, do it man.
Str8 guy jerking for the cam = my kryptonite
U cd split the tips with him.
OMG YES.
Please!!!

Jude gave a rueful chuckle. "Dudes, seriously. If I thought for a minute that he would, I'd ask him tomorrow. But no way."

Why not?
Doesn't hurt to ask.

Shawn found himself wondering the same thing. Why did Jude immediately assume he wouldn't? Did he think he was too straight? Too vanilla? Too *chicken*? He bristled at the implications.

"Yeah, no. He'd think I was hitting on him and would run a mile. Plus, not everyone wants their junk on camera for the world to see, you know. Only exhibitionists like me. Speaking of which… it's getting late, guys, so it's time for me to give you what you're waiting for."

Even though Shawn had already come twice, he was hard again watching Jude finish. Damn, he looked good. There was no other way to describe it. It wasn't so much that Shawn was turned on by watching a guy jerking off rather than watching straight porn or girl-on-girl, it was just that it was so fucking sexy the way Jude got lost in the act. Near the end it was like nobody was watching him at all. Jude closed his eyes, spread his legs, and squeezed his balls, and his whole body jerked as he came with a desperate-sounding moan that made Shawn's toes curl in empathy.

Jude looked tired afterwards, even yawned as he was saying his goodbyes to his viewers.

"Goodnight, guys, till next time." He blew a kiss at the camera and was gone.

Once the illicit thrill of watching Jude was over, Shawn felt flat and lonely. Jerking off to porn was one thing, but jerking off over one of your housemates—one of your friends, because he felt like he could count Jude as a mate now—was quite another. It made Shawn only too aware of what he didn't have at the end of it. Someone to kiss and talk to afterwards; a warm body in his bed to snuggle up to.

After cleaning up and brushing his teeth, Shawn got under the covers. His thoughts turned to Jude again. He wondered how Jude felt after doing one of his shows, whether he felt lonely too. His mind wandered back to the conversation Jude had had with his fans about asking Shawn to join in with one of his shows.

Was it crazy that he felt almost disappointed that Jude wasn't planning on asking him?

This weird crush on Jude was certainly broadening Shawn's horizons.

On Monday after work, Shawn had holed up in his room and took an interesting detour from his usual porn. He searched for gay porn on Tumblr and got lost down a rabbit hole of images, gifs, and video clips. Through his experimental porn-diving he soon found that Jude wasn't the only guy he could get off on watching.

Shawn couldn't decide whether this was a relief or a problem. He wondered how he'd managed to keep this a secret from himself for so long. It was amazing what an effective barrier denial could be. But Jude seemed to have brought those mental blocks crashing down like dominoes.

Lying in bed after jerking off to a video of two guys blowing each other, Shawn considered his options.

A hook-up app seemed the obvious choice if he wanted to take his bi-experimentation to the next level. But he knew for a fact that Jez and Mac still dipped into Grindr occasionally, not to hook up, but to flirt with other guys for fun—usually together. Plus with all the other gay or bi guys Shawn knew: Josh, Rupert, Dev, Ewan, there was way too much chance of someone seeing his profile. Shawn wasn't ready to out himself yet.

He cast his mind back to Jude's show and the comments guys had been making in chat. At first more of a fantasy, a half-formed plan began to take shape. But as the details crystallised, Shawn found himself thinking of it as a legitimate possibility.

Could I?

Of course he could, but the real question was whether he'd have the balls to go through with it.

Shawn left it a couple more days and then watched Jude's Wednesday cam show, and that made up his mind. He had nothing to lose, and Jude could only say no.

So the next evening, he went up to Jude's room and knocked on the door, his heart hammering against his ribs like a battering ram.

"Come in!" Jude called.

"Hey," Shawn said as he entered.

"Oh, hey. You've finally got the hang of that knocking-and-waiting thing, then." Jude grinned, looking up from where he was sitting on his bed with his laptop. He closed the laptop as Shawn came closer.

"Ha-ha."

"Have a seat." Jude gestured to his chair… the chair he sat in while he was doing his shows. Shawn sat, trying not to picture Jude naked there with his dick out—that wouldn't help him focus on what he needed to say. "What's up, man?"

This was it. Shawn needed to get out the words he'd been planning. They'd been running in a loop in his head for the past few days, but now it came to the crunch, his mind blanked out for a moment.

"So... uh, I wanted to ask you about your cam shows. Like, specifically"—he swallowed hard and forced himself not to duck away from Jude's enquiring gaze—"have you ever done a show with another guy? Would your viewers pay more for that?"

Jude narrowed his eyes; his reply was cautious. "Um, no. I've only ever done solo stuff. Why are you asking?"

"Well... I could do with some extra cash. My job doesn't pay well and I'm tired of being in debt. You said how much you earn, and it gave me ideas, that's all. I did some research, and it looks like the whole 'straight guy doing gay stuff for money' is a thing that some people really dig. I thought... maybe you'd be interested in trying that." He hurried out the final part because his face was burning hot now. He swallowed hard again. "With me," he added. As if that wasn't obvious.

Jude's eyes were wide. Shawn could practically see the dollar signs flashing in them, like in a cartoon. "Seriously? Are you fucking kidding me? You'd do that?"

Shawn nodded. "Yep."

"Have you thought it through?" Jude's face turned serious. "It's not something you want to do unless you're sure. I know the Internet is a big place, but there's always a chance someone will find out. People can screen-cap or even rip the video. Once it's out there, there's no taking it back. Are you prepared to take the risk?"

That was something Shawn had already been through in his head. "I'm not planning a career in politics or education. I'll take the chance."

"Okay. Well, if you're sure, then I'm game. It would be a gold mine, I reckon. A lot of my viewers would tip extra to see me getting a straight guy off—unless you just want to jerk off with me, that would be okay too. I mean… it doesn't have to be hands-on." He sounded a little flustered.

"No, it's cool. Hands-on is fine."

Hands-on was *definitely* fine. Shawn would be okay with getting to touch Jude too, but he wasn't sure how to bring that up. One thing at a time.

Jude's cheeks were pink now and Shawn wondered if he was turned on by the conversation. Shawn himself was rocking a semi and hoped it wasn't obvious.

Jude cleared his throat. "Look. Why don't you take until the weekend to think about it? Then, if you're still sure you want to try it, you can join me during my next show on Sunday. We can talk about it beforehand and work out how far you're prepared to go."

"Okay," Shawn agreed. He was pretty sure he wasn't going to change his mind, but maybe Jude needed time. He stood up, tugging his hoodie down to cover his hard-on. "We'll talk at the weekend. Night."

"Goodnight, man."

CHAPTER SIX

Jude's feverish imagination was in overdrive for the rest of the week. He kept replaying his conversation with Shawn in his head and wondering whether he'd dreamed it. Because fuck, the thought of doing a show with Shawn was right up there with all his favourite sexual fantasies.

It wasn't so much a turning-the-straight-guy thing. Jude reckoned that for Shawn to be prepared to do this, he had to be bi-curious at the very least. The idea of being the one to help Shawn work himself out gave Jude a heady feeling of power. He really hoped Shawn wouldn't change his mind.

Jude gave him space, not wanting to push him into anything, but by Saturday night he was starting to wonder whether Shawn was having second thoughts.

Finally, a knock sounded on Jude's door while he was sitting at his desk, working on an assignment. His heart skipped a beat with anticipation. "Come in."

Sure enough, it was Shawn. "Hi." He closed the door behind him and stood there awkwardly.

"Have a seat," Jude gestured to his unmade bed and spun around on his desk chair to face him.

Shawn sat on the edge of the bed. "So... I've, uh, decided I want to do it." He held Jude's gaze, and in those eyes there was a hint of something that looked like a challenge. "Tomorrow."

Excitement rippled through Jude. "Awesome. My viewers will love it. Especially if we tell them you've never done anything with another guy before. Have you thought about what you're prepared to do on camera?"

"Not specifically." Shawn shrugged. "What did you have in mind?"

"Well, first off, are you prepared to show your face? If you're worried about privacy, we could cut your head off with the camera angle, which would make you way less identifiable, but we'd probably get more tips if they can see all of you."

"I don't mind showing my face. We talked about that already."

"Okay, I was just checking. As for the rest... well. We could jerk off together. Or I could jerk you off, or blow you, or a bit of both."

Shawn's face flushed and he shifted on the bed, leaning forward a little and putting his hands in his lap. "Yeah, that sounds fine." He cleared his throat. "Both."

Jude grinned. "Okay, well, we'll start with some jerking off, and then we can switch to me getting you off for the camera. I'm good at it, I promise, and if you get freaked out, you can just close your eyes and pretend I'm a girl."

Shawn gave a nervous chuckle. "Yeah, right."

Jude couldn't tell because of the way Shawn was sitting, but he was pretty sure he was turned on just from the conversation. His cheeks were pink and he seemed to be deliberately hiding his crotch. That was a good sign. Perhaps Shawn had a dash of exhibitionist kink as well as bi-curiosity. If so, it would help keep him horny for the camera tomorrow.

There was an awkward silence between them now, and Jude could think of nothing obvious to fill it with. "I'd better get back to this." He gestured to his laptop and the books spread out on his desk. "I need to get this finished for Monday, and I'll be busy tomorrow night." He gave Shawn a knowing grin.

"Oh yeah, okay. I'll leave you in peace." Shawn stood.

Jude couldn't help glancing down. Poor Shawn had nowhere to hide his boner now—it looked a decent size through his sweatpants. That would be fun to play with tomorrow. "Nice," Jude eyed it approvingly before dragging his gaze up to Shawn's face.

Shawn was still blushing, and he gave a sheepish smile. "Thanks. I guess."

"You should save that for tomorrow. You'll get a better money shot that way."

"But if I don't wank tonight, I might come too quickly."

"Oh, don't worry about that," Jude said smoothly. "I won't let you come till I'm ready."

Shawn's eyes darkened and a muscle ticked in his jaw. "Right." He cleared his throat. "Okay, then. Good luck with the studying." He hurried to the door and was gone.

Jude chuckled. It was fun seeing Shawn flustered. *Tomorrow is going to be awesome.*

Jude had arranged for Shawn to come up to his room about fifteen minutes before they were due to start. He wanted to work out the best place for them to film and get the lighting right. The obvious place was side-by-side on the bed, but he'd need to move his desk alongside for his laptop to stand on.

When Shawn turned up exactly on time, cheeks pink and hair still damp from the shower, Jude got up and let him in.

"Hi," he said.

"Hey." Jude locked the door behind him. "You okay?" Shawn had the look of a man about to face a firing squad rather than one about to get his dick sucked.

"Yeah." Shawn's voice was tight.

"Don't worry, I'll be gentle with you—unless you want me to be rough?" He waggled his eyebrows, trying to lighten the serious mood.

"Very funny," Shawn huffed, but he gave a small grin and the tension in his shoulders eased a little.

"Okay." Jude became all business. Keeping Shawn busy would stop him getting nervous. "Give me a hand moving the desk. If we put it here"—he pointed—"then my laptop can stand on it. That should give a better angle than putting it on a chair, and it will fit both of us in if we're sitting on the bed."

The desk was heavy, but easy enough to move with the two of them. Shawn's biceps bulged and veins corded in his forearms as he lifted it.

"Perfect," Jude said. "Now come and sit on the bed while I check this is gonna work."

Shawn took a seat. Jude had already set the bed up with the pillows against the wall to make it look more like a sofa. The bed was a double, so even with pillows behind them, they could still stretch their legs out. Shawn adjusted a pillow before leaning back, trying and failing to look casual.

Resisting the urge to tease him again, Jude stuck to getting things organised. Shawn would loosen up soon enough. Jude remembered how nervous he'd been his first time doing this, and he'd only been jerking off for the camera. On top of that, Jude suspected this was Shawn's first time doing anything with another guy. No wonder he was jumpy.

Jude set the webcam up and angled it so he could see Shawn on the bed, plus the space beside him.

"Is it running?" Shawn sounded alarmed.
"Not yet."

Jude came to sit beside Shawn, moving in close so their shoulders touched and he could feel the warmth of Shawn's body through their T-shirts. He looked critically at the screen, then leaned forward to change the angle slightly. "That's better. They'll be able to see our faces and our dicks now. All the important bits." He frowned. "It's a bit dark, though. I don't think the lamps are enough." He got up and flicked the switch by the door, flooding the room with bright white light.

"Isn't that a bit much?" Shawn asked nervously.

"Nope." Jude sat beside him again. They were much clearer on the laptop screen. "The guys watching will complain if the picture is too dark. They'll want to see as much as they can." Shawn didn't reply. "Hey." Jude put a hand on Shawn's thigh, feeling hard muscle under the fabric. "It's not too late to change your mind."

As much as he wanted to do this with Shawn, he didn't want to do it unless Shawn was sure.

"Nah, it's fine. I'm just nervous. I want to get it over with."

"That's really not good for my ego, man. Just saying." He patted Shawn's leg before pulling his hand away. He'd tried to keep his voice light, but a part of him stung at Shawn's words. Shawn made it sound like a chore, or worse, something horrible, like going to the dentist.

"I didn't mean it like that. Fuck." Shawn rubbed the back of his neck and sighed. "It's just a big deal for me, okay? You know I've never done anything like this before."

Jude wondered whether he meant being with another man or being on camera, or both. But he didn't ask; he supposed they were all big things, and together they made a really big deal. "Yeah. It's okay. I get it."

A glance at the clock showed Jude it was nearly time. Two minutes to go. "Oh, I just realised we need to know what to call each other. My viewers know me as Tom. What do you want your alter ego to be called?"

"Fuck, um, I dunno."

"What about Chris? You look a bit like Captain America."

"I do?"

"Yeah, you know"—Jude waved his hands vaguely—"Short blond hair, killer abs."

"Yeah, okay. Chris is fine."

"He really *is* fine."

Shawn chuckled. "I'll take that as a compliment."

"You should. Okay, are you ready to get this show on the road?"

Shawn's response was immediate and sure. "Yep."

"Right, then. Let's go, Chris."

Jude patted him on the thigh again and then reached for the wireless mouse on the chair beside him; he clicked the button to start the show.

And like flipping a switch, Jude was in showman mode. "Good evening boys… and girls, I know there are a few of you out there too." He winked and grinned invitingly at the camera as he ran a hand through his dark curls.

Immediately the chat box started filling with messages.

Hey hottie.
Hi Tom, who's ur friend?
Why are there two of you?

"I have something special planned for you tonight." Jude squeezed Shawn's leg. "Let me introduce you to my mate, Chris. Say hi to my fans, Chris. After tonight they might be your fans too."

"Um, hi." Shawn gave a goofy little wave and a nervous grin.

The chat box exploded with greetings.

"He's really nervous," Jude told them, "because this is his first time on camera…." He let his voice trail off seductively for a moment and moved his hand a little higher on Shawn's thigh. "But not only that. This is also the first time he's done anything with another guy. Isn't that right, man?"

"Yeah." Shawn's voice was husky. He coughed and said more clearly, "Yeah, that's right, Tom."

Fuck
Holy shit that's hot
Lucky you
I wanna blow him

Jude chuckled. "Yeah, I wanna blow him too—and he says that's okay. Poor Chris here just broke up with his girlfriend, so he needs a little TLC." Shawn's thigh tensed under Jude's hand and he hoped he hadn't overstepped. He was playing this up for the camera, and the guys in the chat window were lapping it up.

With his free hand, Jude adjusted his cock, which was starting to get hard already. He glanced at Shawn's lap, but his bulge looked soft. It was high time to change that.

Jude started to play with himself more obviously, rubbing his dick through the soft football shorts he was wearing. He was going commando today, and the fabric tented as his erection rose. "I'm horny already, just thinking about getting my mouth on Chris's cock. Can't wait to find out what he tastes like. Are you gonna make it hard for me, man?" He nudged Shawn.

"I bet the guys watching wouldn't mind a peek at it soon."

Shawn didn't answer, but Jude caught the movement of his hand out of the corner of his eye and turned to watch as Shawn started to squeeze his dick.

"Yeah, that's it."

Jude watched as Shawn thickened, easy to see through his sweatpants. The sight of it sent a jolt of heat to his groin, a feedback loop of desire. Jude was hard all the way now and his hand felt good, but he wanted skin on skin. "Don't forget to tip, guys. Twenty quid, shirts off, but you need to get to fifty before we show you the goods. Two for the price of one tonight."

That reminder took the tips to twenty fast.

"Okay, the shirts come off."

Take each others off, someone immediately said in chat, and others agreed. *Yeah. That wd be hot.*

"What do you reckon, Chris?" Jude asked. "Can I take your shirt off for you?"

"Yeah, okay."

"Come here, then." Jude knelt up, making sure his body was in shot.

Shawn moved to face him, also rising to his knees.

"Nice tents, yes?" Jude looked down between them where their erections were hard and obvious, distorting the fabric of their clothes. When he moved his gaze back up to Shawn's face, Shawn had flushed, his pupils dark. Jude lifted the hem of Shawn's shirt and tugged, and Shawn raised his arms obligingly as Jude slid the T-shirt up and off. Shawn's mostly hairless chest was still a light tan from the summer and his skin looked smooth. His nipples were tight. Jude's mouth watered with the urge to lick.

"Shit, man," he muttered, for Shawn as much as for the camera, "you're so hot. Can I touch you?"

"Yeah."

"God." Jude ran his hands up Shawn's abs to his chest, deliberately skimming the nipples with his palms and making Shawn shiver. He gripped Shawn's shoulders hard, squeezing the muscles. "Hot. As. Fuck."

Shawn's eyes burned into his, but the expression was hard to read.

Jude suddenly remembered the camera was on them. In the heat of the moment, he'd almost forgotten this was a show and not a hook-up. Shawn was only doing this for the money, not because he wanted Jude.

Jude was nothing if not professional. He squashed down the twinge of disappointment and stripped off his own T-shirt, tossing it aside. It landed on top of Shawn's on the floor.

"You want to touch me too?" he asked lightly. "No pressure, man. But if you want to, I'm all yours."

Shawn hesitated, tension in every part of him. Then he sighed. Something shifted as if at the flip of a switch, and he gave himself up to the moment. He lifted his hands and put them on Jude's chest, tentatively stroking his fingertips through the hair there. He said huskily, "Feels weird."

"No tits and more hair than you're used to?" Jude grinned. "I can see how this would be a bit different."

Shawn moved his hands more confidently, flattening them and mapping out the planes of Jude's chest, the width of his ribcage. Shawn was more muscular than Jude, but Jude was big-boned, so they weren't very different in size overall. "You feel good," he finally said. It was hard to tell whether he meant it or whether it was just for the camera.

Speaking of the camera, Jude hadn't been paying attention to the chat window. "Let's sit back down and see what these guys think of you so far."

They settled back down on the bed. Jude deliberately spread his thighs wider than before so his knee touched Shawn's leg.

Predictably, the chat had gone wild. Jude scrolled up a little and chuckled as he caught up with the comments. "Looks like they like you, Chris. And holy shit, we've flown past fifty quid in tips already. Thanks, guys!"

That was unheard of so early in a show. If things carried on like that, they were going to make a lot of money tonight. The counter was still going up.

Jude nudged Shawn. "Okay, are you ready to show me and the viewers what you're packing?" His pulse surged with anticipation, as eager for a look as the guys out there on the Internet.

"Yeah. I guess so," Shawn replied.

CHAPTER SEVEN

Shawn swallowed, his mouth dry with nerves. He wondered why he'd thought it was a good idea to try this out on camera. If he'd been honest with Jude and just told him he wanted experience with a guy, maybe they could have done this without—he glanced at the view counter—over five hundred people watching. *Jesus.* His dick was hard under his hand, though, clearly turned on by this fucked-up situation. He wasn't sure what that said about him and didn't want to think about it right now.

"On a count of three?" Jude asked.

Shawn glanced sideways. "Okay."

Jude gave him a reassuring grin and then dropped his gaze to Shawn's lap, but Shawn kept his eyes on Jude's face, wanting to see his reaction when he bared himself.

"One, two, three, go!"

Shawn pushed his sweats down, freeing his erection. The skin was hot in his palm and his foreskin had drawn back. His hissed as his dry palm stroked the sensitive head.

"Nice dick, man." Jude watched intently. "Really fucking nice." He licked his lips and Shawn could almost feel it like an extra touch, imagining how Jude's mouth would feel on him, how it was going to feel on him later. He squeezed himself harder at the thought, slowing his stroke to keep himself from getting too close.

Shawn let his gaze slide down to Jude's cock, finally seeing it in the flesh with time to appreciate it. It was impressive, and Shawn felt a flash of envy along with desire. Jude was longer and thicker than he was—not that Shawn was lacking in the dick department, but he didn't quite measure up to Jude.

Jude pumped himself slowly and Shawn watched the movement, matching it with his own hand on himself. When he dragged his gaze back to Jude's face, their eyes met. Shawn's cheeks heated and he looked away quickly, wondering what Jude could read in his expression. He felt vulnerable, exposed in more than just a physical way.

They jerked off for a couple of minutes in silence. The tension was already coiling tight in Shawn's balls so he paced himself, careful not to take things too far.

"Are you ready for more?" Jude asked.

"I think so."

Jude chuckled. "I was talking to the guys out there, actually. But good to know you're on board, man."

Fuck. Shawn's toes curled with embarrassment. "Sorry."

Jude pressed his knee against Shawn's reassuringly. "Nothing to be sorry about," he murmured quietly. Then he said in a louder voice, "So who wants to see me get Chris off? He said I can use my hands, and maybe my mouth. If you'd like to make that happen for him, we need more tips first."

The chat box was going crazy now. It was impossible to keep up with the comments. But most of them seemed to be approving or complimentary. Shawn gave up trying to read them. Jude seemed to be in control of this, and he was the expert, after all.

"Okay, okay. I'll get naked," Jude said, presumably in reply to a comment. "You too, Chris?"

"Uh. Yeah."

They raised their hips in tandem to slide off the rest of their clothes. Shawn glanced sideways to check out Jude again. Dark pubes, with heavy balls hanging below that amazing cock. He looked even better in the flesh than he did on camera.

By the time they settled back down, the tips had passed one hundred.

"So, it's time to get hands-on. How are we gonna do this?" Jude asked.

Shawn snorted. "If you need me to show you, then you're less experienced than I thought." The bravado was to cover his nerves, which had ratcheted up at the thought of Jude touching him. It was a relief in a way, because the anxiety took the edge off his need to come. One of Shawn's fears was of coming as soon as Jude laid a hand on him. Hopefully that wouldn't happen while he was feeling so tense.

Jude gave a surprised huff of laughter. "Hey, less of the sass. I meant how we're gonna work it so the guys at home get a good view."

Shawn shrugged. "Like this works for now."

"Okay, then. In that case, let me help you out with that."

And with no further ado, Jude twisted around to sit cross-legged with his side to the camera. He reached for Shawn's dick, batting Shawn's hand away so he could curl his fingers around him and stroke.

Shawn felt it like a jolt of electricity. Not that it was very different to his own hand, but the sight of it, the knowledge that it was another guy's hand on his cock was overwhelming. It felt good, shockingly good as Jude's strong fingers and slightly calloused palm slid over his sensitive skin. The weirdest part, though, was how right it felt. Shawn had been expecting to feel something like guilt, or maybe shame, because he'd suppressed these desires for years. But nothing about this felt wrong. He clenched his fists where they lay resting on his thighs and bit his lip.

"Does that feel good?" Jude asked after a few strokes.

"Yeah," Shawn managed, his voice a breathy gasp.

"How do you like it? Fast? Slow? Is this enough pressure?"

"Uh…." It was hard to think with Jude stroking him. "Like this is good. Slow—for now."

Jude used his louder voice for the camera again. "I hope you guys at home are enjoying this. I can't keep up with chat while I'm focusing on my mate here, so I'm sorry to neglect you. But I'm sure you can find ways of keeping yourselves occupied while you watch." His tone turned intimate again. "Hey, dude. You okay there? If you bite that lip any harder, you're gonna draw blood."

Shawn laughed, amusement making him relax a little.

Jude stroked a little harder. "That's better."

But now that Shawn's nerves were dissipating, his orgasm was already starting to build. He tried to fight it down, not wanting to admit he was embarrassingly close already.

But it was a battle he'd never win. "Stop!" he bit out, muscles tensing.

Jude froze, hand gripping tightly. "What's up?"

"Just… getting close. I need you to slow down a little."

"Yeah?"

Shawn glanced sideways and saw Jude's smile. "There's no need to look so smug about it."

Jude's grin widened. "Yeah. Well. Anyway, you're in good hands. I'm an expert in delayed gratification. So just sit back and trust me. But tell me when you need a time out, okay?"

"Okay." Shawn let his shoulders drop and uncurled his fists. He took a deep breath. "Carry on."

But Jude had taken him at his word when Shawn had asked him to slow down. He moved his hand to cup Shawn's balls instead, testing the weight of them in his palm and squeezing lightly. Then he stopped. "This isn't very comfortable for me. Let's change this a little. You try lying back against the headboard. Prop yourself up on some pillows so the guys can still see your face as well as the goods."

Shawn complied while Jude rearranged the laptop so they'd both still be in shot. Then he got onto the bed and kneeled astride Shawn's legs.

"That's better." Jude wrapped his hand around Shawn's erection again and ran his thumb over the slit, smearing precome around.

It was better for Shawn like this. Comfortable and relaxed, he was able to focus on the sensation of Jude's hand. The view was good too. Jude loomed over him, big and strong. The weight of him on Shawn's thighs, the scratch of his leg hair, everything about him screamed *male* and Shawn found he was completely okay with that.

Jude stroked him slowly, lightly, with tantalisingly not enough pressure. But that was perfect because Shawn was so close to the edge.

"Fuck," he muttered.

Jude's hand slowed. "You okay?"

"Yeah, don't stop. It's good."

"Don't be afraid to make some noise. I think the people watching would like to hear you."

With that permission—and knowing that Dev was round at Ewan's tonight, so nobody would overhear—Shawn stopped holding back. He didn't need to be embarrassed to show how much he was enjoying this; he could always pretend he was putting it on for the camera.

At the next slide of Jude's hand, he let out a little moan and shifted his body, trying to thrust into Jude's fist, but Jude's weight kept him pinned. Shawn liked that too, the feeling that Jude was strong enough to hold him down, to make him keep still and take it.

"You need to be patient." Jude's smile was dirty and his grip tightened.

Something cool touched Shawn's thigh and he looked down to see that Jude's cock was leaking precome, connecting them with a glistening strand. Without pausing to think about what he was doing, he reached down and caught it on his finger. Jude's cock jerked.

"You wanna taste it? I dare you."

Shawn never backed down from a challenge. He held Jude's gaze as he put his finger in his mouth and sucked it clean. Jude's eyes burned into him, dark and hungry and an answering heat curled in the pit of Shawn's belly.

"You're pretty eager for a straight boy."

I'm not straight.

As soon as the words formed in Shawn's head, he knew them to be true. He wasn't straight. He'd never been straight. He enjoyed sex with women, but he'd used that as a shield because he hadn't wanted to admit he was attracted to guys too. But with Jude pinning him to the bed and the taste of him on his tongue, he had nowhere to hide from his desire any more. He wasn't quite ready to say it out loud though. Instead he raised his eyebrows and said, "So, are you gonna blow me, or what?"

"Getting desperate?" Jude gave him a dirty grin.

"Just looking forward to experiencing those awesome skills you told me about."

"Right, then."

Jude adjusted his position, kneeing Shawn's thighs apart so he could settle between them. He glanced sideways quickly, which reminded Shawn they were still on camera. Shawn turned his head too and paused to admire the picture they made. They looked good together, and the sight of it made Shawn even hornier.

"You ready for this, guys?" Jude asked the camera. "I think Chris is."

Shawn looked at the chat window.

Fuck yeah.

Str8 dick FTW.

Blow his mind.

Wish I cd taste him.

Then the wet heat of Jude's mouth closed around the tip of his cock and Shawn lost the ability to read or think about anything other than what Jude was doing to him.

"*Fuck*," he hissed, curling his hands into the duvet to stop himself reaching for Jude's hair. "Yeah, suck it."

Jude obliged and Shawn turned his attention away from the screen to his own personal live porn show that was going on between his thighs. Jude's cheeks hollowed as he sucked Shawn deep and flicked his gaze up to meet Shawn's own. He bobbed up and down a few times, gagging a little as Shawn hit the back of his throat.

Shawn lost all track of time as Jude played his body like an instrument. He seemed to know instinctively when Shawn was getting close, and he often backed off before Shawn needed to warn him. After the first couple of times that happened, Shawn lost any residual self-consciousness and forgot they were being watched. His focus narrowed down to the ache in his cock and the burning need to come. Every time the chance was snatched away from him, he drifted a little farther from reality.

In between sucking him and driving him to the brink, Jude pulled off and licked Shawn's balls instead or massaged his thighs. He kept checking in with him, using a low, intimate voice that felt as though it was for Shawn, not the camera—"Are you doing okay?" or "Still with me?"

After a particularly close call when he pushed Jude away with an urgent "Stop! I'm close," Jude moved to straddle Shawn again. He leaned over him, his face close. Their cocks aligned and Shawn lifted his hips without thinking, trying to grind up against him, desperate to feel more of Jude's body in contact with his own.

"God, you're so into this, aren't you?" Jude's breath was warm on Shawn's lips and his voice barely more than a whisper; there was no way the webcam would pick it up.

"Yeah," Shawn gasped, past caring about what he was admitting to, "but I wanna come."

Jude huffed a soft laugh. "Soon." He patted Shawn's cheek and then drew back, letting his hand slide down Shawn's neck and over his chest and abs until he wrapped it tight around Shawn's cock again—not stroking, just holding him.

"You're killing me," Shawn managed weakly.

"But you love it." Then Jude turned to look at the camera and raised his voice. "Chris is getting desperate, guys. Do you think I should let him come soon?"

Shawn glanced at the chat; most of the guys seemed to be voting yes. *Thank fuck*. His balls might explode if he had to wait too much longer.

"Yeah. I think he deserves it too." Jude started jerking him then, his hand tight and perfect as it slid Shawn's foreskin back and forth over the head with every stroke. Shawn's whole body tensed in anticipation, every cell primed and ready to blow.

Shawn moaned, "Oh fuck yeah, like that. *Yes.*" But just as he was there, almost at the point of no return, Jude stopped and took his hand away.

Shawn's cock jerked hopelessly, straining against thin air. "You bastard! You fucking cockteasing *arsehole!*"

Done with waiting, he reached down to stroke himself. He wanted to roll Jude over and come all over his smug face—

But Jude was too quick for him. "No you don't." He grabbed Shawn's wrists and pinned them to the bed by his side. "Maybe I should have tied you up." Shawn's breath caught in an audible gasp and his cock jerked again. Jude raised his eyebrows, a knowing look spreading over his face. "Oh. You'd like that, wouldn't you?"

Shawn glared furiously at him, not prepared to admit how that thought had turned him on like fire in his veins. The idea of being bound and helpless while Jude did this to him was almost enough to make him come right there without a hand or mouth on him. "Fuck you," he gritted out.

Jude backed off then, releasing Shawn's wrists and taking his cock in hand again. "Maybe another time," he said lightly. He stroked, slowly at first, until Shawn growled and thrust into his hand. "You'd look so hot tied up, maybe to a chair. And I could take my time with you and you couldn't do anything about it."

Jude's voice was like a drug; the images he conjured curled into Shawn's brain like smoke.

"Don't stop," he pleaded, and he wasn't sure whether he was talking about the movement of Jude's hand or the fantasies his voice was creating.

"You'd just have to take what I gave you and be grateful for it."

Shawn's body jerked and he arched off the bed with a strangled cry. His climax tore through him, muscles tensing and releasing as he came and came until he was weak and limp.

The pat of Jude's hand on his hip brought Shawn back to earth. Jude's smile was soft, and it made Shawn's stomach do a little flip.

"Wow, that's a lot of jizz." Jude ran his fingers through the mess on Shawn's belly and held them up for the camera.

Shawn chuckled, unable to muster up the energy to move, wrung out like a wet dishcloth. "Yeah, well. That's what you get when you tease me for that long."

"Good to know." Still kneeling astride Shawn's thighs, Jude wrapped his sticky hand around his own erection. "You're not the only one who's been waiting to come, though. And you look good like that. Is it okay if I jerk off over you? You're already a mess, so I might as well."

That idea made Shawn feel hot all over—in a good way. He suspected Jude was playing to the camera again. His tone was light and teasing, but his dick was hard and flushed with blood. He was obviously turned on, regardless of what was for the audience and what might be real.

"Yeah, go for it." Shawn put his elbows on the bed and propped himself up to watch. His stomach tensed at the movement and come pooled in the dips between the muscles.

Jude didn't waste any time. His gaze roved over Shawn as he stroked himself hard and fast. He was looking at Shawn's body rather than his face, lingering on Shawn's nipples, the come on his belly, and his softening cock. Shawn couldn't tear his gaze away from Jude's face; the naked desire there made him feel powerful.

Jude wants me.

He wondered what Jude would like to do to him if he knew that Shawn would let him do pretty much anything now the floodgates of his sexual discovery were open. He imagined what Jude's dick would feel like in his hand, in his mouth, and it scared him how much he wanted to find out.

Jude's breathing was harsh now and Shawn knew he wasn't going to take long. He gasped and tensed, eyes fluttering shut for a moment as he came. Warm spurts hit Shawn's stomach, mingling with his own cooling release. When Jude was done, he sagged forward, supporting his weight with his hands, head hanging low. His curls tumbled forward and a stray lock tickled Shawn's face. Without thinking, Shawn tucked it behind Jude's ear.

Jude snapped his eyes open and they gazed at each other for a moment. Jude licked his lips. Shawn fought down a powerful urge to kiss him as silence stretched between them until it became uncomfortable.

When Jude finally pulled away to reach for tissues, Shawn sighed in relief.

Grinning at the camera as he wiped his hands, Jude said, "Well, guys, I hope you're all satisfied with what we showed you tonight. Thanks for all the tips. You've been very generous." He passed the box of tissues to Shawn. "Maybe I'll be able to get Chris to join me again. I'm definitely gonna try. What do you reckon, mate?" He squeezed Shawn's thigh.

Shawn felt a thrill of excitement. "Maybe." He wouldn't take much persuading, but he wanted to tease the guys online.

"Okay, time for us to say goodbye. Till next time…." Jude leaned over to reach the mouse, and with a click, the camera feed went blank.

Silence descended like an uncomfortable, scratchy blanket.

Shawn's skin felt tight and hot, and he suddenly felt way too naked and exposed. The urge to flee rolled through him, making his stomach lurch. "Get your hairy arse off me," he said roughly.

Jude moved, standing and stretching, making no effort to reach for his clothes.

Shawn sat up and hunched over himself protectively as he wiped his stomach with a handful of tissues. It came off pretty easily there, but there was some spunk stuck in his pubes that would take a shower to fix. He picked up his shorts and pulled them back on, feeling immediately better for being covered up. "Put some fucking clothes on, dude. I don't need to see that now we're done."

He tried to make it sound like a joke, but his voice came out too harsh. Raw, like his nerves.

Jude raised an eyebrow but didn't comment. He picked up his shorts and stepped into them.

Shawn looked up and got an eyeful of his Jude's arse as he pulled them up, and damn if that didn't make his heart beat faster. Now this experiment was over, he wished he'd touched Jude too instead of just lying there and taking it. It didn't feel like he'd pushed out of his comfort zone far enough. He hadn't done anything tonight that he hadn't done with girls before. It still felt different, though.

He stood and put on his T-shirt. "I need a shower," he announced. "So I'm gonna go."

Jude reached out and put a hand on Shawn's arm. Jude's palm was hot, like a brand on his skin. "Hang on a minute. We need to work out how I pay you your share. Do you have a PayPal account?"

Shawn blinked. He'd forgotten that this was supposed to be about money. "Oh, uh… yeah. Let me write down my email address."

Jude gave him a piece of paper and a pen, and Shawn stooped to rest on the desk while he wrote.

"There you go."

"Thanks." Jude put his hands in his pockets. "So, um, do you want to try it again sometime? We made more than twice what I'd usually earn for a show, so you'd be doing me a favour."

Shawn paused for a beat. He wanted to agree immediately but was afraid of sounding too keen. "Can I think about it?" he asked instead.

"Course." Jude gave a small smile. "Let me know when you've decided. There's no rush. Night, then."

"Night." Shawn hurried to the door and escaped, eager to be alone with his whirling, confusing thoughts.

The only thing he was sure of was that he *definitely* wanted to do that again. As soon as possible.

CHAPTER EIGHT

Jude didn't see Shawn until the following evening. He felt weirdly nervous about facing him after the night before. The sex had been amazing, but having the camera on them confused things, making it hard to gauge how much of Shawn's reaction was genuine and what was put on for show. He'd clearly been turned on, totally into what Jude had done to him from a physical point of view, but Jude couldn't tell how it had affected him emotionally. After they were done, Shawn had scarpered almost immediately, which didn't seem like a good sign.

Jude hoped Shawn wasn't freaking out too much and that things weren't going to be weird between them.

He was playing *Mario Kart* with Jez and Mac in the living room when Shawn came in with a plate of food.

Jude tensed, searching Shawn's face for any embarrassment or discomfort.

Shawn didn't meet his gaze. "Alright," he said as he made his way over to the table.

"Hey, Shawny," Jez said cheerily. "How's it going?"

Jude and Mac added their greetings too.

"Pretty good, thanks."

Shawn sounded fairly chilled, so Jude relaxed a little.

They carried on with their game while Shawn ate. Jez and Mac filled the silence with their usual teasing and trash talk. Honestly, they were like a pair of giant kids when they were gaming. The way they got all competitive and pissy with each other was like a weird form of foreplay.

"Hey, you wanna play, Shawn?" Jez asked. "You can join in the next round if you're done eating."

"Sure."

Shawn joined them on the sofa when he was ready to start. Jude budged up next to Mac to make space for Shawn beside him. It was cosy, their knees and elbows bumped, and he was very aware of the warmth of Shawn's body in all the places they touched.

They played a few rounds, and by then it was clear that Jez and Mac heckling each other was definitely foreplay.

"Hey!" Mac yelled. "That's cheating."

Jude looked over and laughed when he saw Jez steering one-handed, his other hand in Mac's lap as their on-screen characters raced towards the finish line. At that point Mac's kart went over a cliff into the water.

"You wanker!"

Mac tossed down his controller and straddled Jez, who tried valiantly to carry on playing, but with Mac blocking his view, it was impossible. His kart plunged off the track too. Shawn zoomed past them both to win the race. Jude was too busy laughing at Mac and Jez to care.

Mac had Jez's hands pinned and was trying to look cross with a wriggling, laughing Jez. "You little shit," Mac growled.

"Yeah. But I'm *your* little shit."

Mac's face softened further. "It's a good thing I love you."

The sexual tension between them was palpable, as well as the affection. It turned a twist of longing in Jude's chest like a key in a door. It must be nice having a relationship like that—they were so obviously crazy about each other.

Jez gave Mac a dirty grin. "Take me upstairs and I'll make it up to you."

"For fuck's sake, you two," Shawn complained. "Can you just stop?"

"Oh, sorry, Shawny. Are we being too queer for you again? Offending your delicate straight sensibilities?"

"It's not about you being queer," Shawn said gruffly.

"Are you sure?" Jez's voice had an edge to it. "Because it usually is."

Jude felt an unexpected surge of defensiveness on Shawn's behalf. "Give him a break. He apologised for that. Anyway, I'm queer as fuck and I don't need to see this either. You're just rubbing our poor single noses in your happy togetherness." He kept his voice light.

"Oh." Jez deflated. "Yeah, well. We're gonna take this to our room anyway." He pushed at Mac, who climbed off him and then gave Jez a hand and pulled him up. "Come on, babe. Night, guys."

"Night," Jude and Shawn said in unison.

Shawn sighed when the door closed behind them. "Thanks."

"No worries. You wanna play some more?"

It was good doing something normal with Shawn. Hanging out like friends was easing some of the tension in Jude's chest. He was glad that things weren't weird, despite what they'd done together the night before.

"Yeah."

They set up a two-player race and focused on the game for a while.

Jude was still aware of Shawn beside him. Neither of them had moved despite having more room on the sofa now, and Jude liked the feeling of Shawn sitting close. It made him feel warm and contented, and a little horny, if he was honest, because it was difficult not to think about Shawn naked and desperate. But he managed to keep a lid on it and not embarrass himself.

After several games, Shawn started to yawn and eventually put down his controller. "I need to head to bed soon." He flopped against the back of the sofa.

Jude turned around and shuffled back to sit against the arm of the sofa with his feet up, putting a little distance between them, but now able to see Shawn's face as they talked. "Long day at work?"

"Yeah. And I didn't sleep too well last night." Shawn flushed as soon as the words were out of his mouth.

"Lots on your mind?" Jude asked casually. A sexuality crisis did that to a guy.

Shawn gave a sheepish smile. "You could say that." He looked down at his hands, lacing his fingers together and squeezing till they cracked. "So I, um, I want to do it again. If you do? The webcam thing." He added the last few words as an afterthought, as if he were worried that Jude might not understand.

Jude fought back a grin of delight. He didn't want to look too keen. "Yeah, of course. It benefits both of us, so that's fine with me."

Shawn didn't need to know that Jude's motivations were a little more than financial. But it wasn't as if Shawn hadn't enjoyed himself. It had been clear that no matter how confused he might be, he'd been seriously into what they did together. Shawn's rational mind might not have caught up with his body yet, but that was Shawn's problem, not Jude's.

Shawn broke Jude's train of thought. "So I could join you for your next show on Wednesday?"

Jude frowned for a moment. He didn't remember discussing his schedule with Shawn in that much detail. Maybe he'd mentioned it at the end of the last show? He often did, so that must be it. "Okay. Sounds good."

"Cool." Shawn stood.

"Night, then." Jude let his gaze slide down Shawn's body to the soft bulge in his sweatpants, then admired the curve of his arse as he walked to the door.

"Night." Shawn glanced over his shoulder and totally busted Jude for ogling.

Jude snapped his gaze up milliseconds too late. Shawn gave him a knowing grin.

Cocky fucker.

It was good that Shawn didn't seem to mind Jude's attention, because he'd definitely captured it.

The Wednesday session went much like the Sunday one. They stuck to the same premise. Jude, aka Tom, was "helping out" his mate, Chris, after his girl had dumped him. They kept up the charade that "Chris" was straight and not into guys, even though it was blindingly obvious that being around Jude made Shawn as horny as fuck. It became increasingly obvious that Shawn got off on being dominated, and Jude wondered whether he'd ever explored that with the women he'd slept with.

When they got to the point of Jude jerking Shawn off, he kept stopping and starting, teasing Shawn and driving him crazy.

Shawn tried to touch himself again.

"Seriously, man. You want me to tie you up? 'Cause I will." Jude held Shawn's wrists tightly. Shawn was lying back with his head on the pillow while Jude straddled him. Both of them were naked.

Shawn's cheeks flushed and he bit his lip and shook his head. "No." His arms went limp in Jude's grip as he capitulated, letting Jude raise them over his head and press them down against the mattress.

"You'd look good tied up, though. We should try it sometime. If you'd be up for that?"

"Maybe." Shawn's ribs lifted as he took a breath. His nipples were hard and pointed.

"Well, for tonight let's try something else. Tuck your hands under the pillow and keep them there. If they move, I stop what I'm doing. Are you okay with that?"

Shawn's pupils expanded and he licked his lips before answering breathlessly. "Yeah." He slid his hands beneath the pillow, gaze fixed on Jude.

Jude rewarded him with a smile. "Good." He lowered his head and ran his tongue over one of Shawn's nipples. Shawn tensed, but he didn't move. Jude sucked and Shawn hissed, body jerking. But his hands stayed put. "*Very* good."

Jude crawled backwards. Settling between Shawn's thighs, he licked a hot stripe up from his balls to the tip of his cock. "Now stay like that. I'm gonna drive you crazy."

After they were done, Jude took the initiative. "So, do you want to do this again on Sunday?" he asked as Shawn pulled on his T-shirt.

"Yeah," Shawn said immediately. His cheeks were still flushed from coming and he ran a hand through his hair.

"Cool."

Jude resisted the urge to question him about his motivations, although he was undeniably intrigued. He didn't think it was his business, and talking about feelings would run the risk of making things complicated. He was more than happy to help Shawn figure out the physical side of things, but he wasn't interested in getting deep and meaningful about it.

After Shawn had gone, Jude got ready for bed, then lay and thought about Shawn as he waited for sleep.

The part that fascinated him the most, more than Shawn's bi-curiosity, was the way he responded to Jude taking charge. It was clear that he loved it, loved Jude edging him and making him wait, and he seemed to get a massive thrill out of giving Jude that power over him. Shawn pushed the boundaries, getting impatient sometimes, but when Jude was firm with him and reminded him who was boss, he backed down immediately.

Jude really got off on it too. It wasn't new to him; he'd played around with this type of D/s dynamic with a previous boyfriend, although in that relationship it had been experimental on both sides and they'd switched around, taking turns to be the dominant one. Jude had been okay with that; he was quite versatile in the bedroom. But with Shawn, being in charge felt totally right. He couldn't imagine switching roles.

On Friday evening they went to the gym together again. Shawn still hadn't bought a new membership, but as it was another rainy day, he readily agreed to join Jude when he suggested it. They jogged there, then did a good session of weights before some interval training on the treadmills. After that, they stretched and did some abs work on the mats. It was getting late and the gym was quiet. They could hear a couple of people on the treadmills, but they had this little corner of the gym all to themselves.

"Come on, give me ten more." Jude was holding Shawn's feet and goading him while he suffered through another set of crunches while holding a medicine ball.

"Can't," Shawn grunted, his face dark red with exertion.

"Yes you can. Show me what you're made of."

Shawn huffed his way through them, counting down towards zero as he went. When he got to three, he groaned and lay back panting. "I'm done."

"No, you're not!" Without thinking, Jude slapped Shawn's thigh on the bare skin below his shorts. He did it harder than he meant to. The sound was loud and Shawn jerked in surprise.

"Oi!" Shawn lifted his head off the mat and glared at Jude. But there was something other than anger on his face, and his eyes were dark.

Oh... Jude slapped him again, holding his gaze in challenge. "Do it. Two more."

Shawn gritted his teeth and forced his unwilling body up, muscles straining and tendons popping in his neck. "Wanker," he muttered when he was nearly nose-to-nose with Jude.

"Yep." Jude grinned, watching Shawn lower himself again and then go into the final crunch.

"I hate you."

"No you don't."

Shawn let the medicine ball drop to the mat between his knees and collapsed back, hands on his stomach, a telltale bulge in his shorts. "No," he said quietly, "I don't."

Jude still had his hands on Shawn's ankles. His heart was thumping harder than was warranted given that Shawn had been the one doing the crunches. He patted Shawn's thigh gently this time. "Well done. Now shift your arse. It's my turn to suffer."

As they jogged back to the house, they passed a pizza shop, and the smell wafting out of the door as another customer opened it had Jude's mouth watering. "You got plans for dinner?" he asked.

"No."

"I owe you a dinner, remember? But I'm crap at cooking, so how about I treat you to pizza instead?"

"You don't need to do that," Shawn protested.

Jude had made up his mind. "I want to. Come on." He marched through the doors into the warmth of the shop. The delicious aroma of garlic and baking pizzas made his stomach growl with hunger. He turned to Shawn. "What toppings do you like? We could get a big one to share, and some garlic bread."

They ended up agreeing on a chicken, bacon, and mushroom pizza and bought some Coke to drink while they were waiting. The shop was mainly geared towards takeaway, so there were only a couple of small plastic tables and chairs. But as it was early in the evening and nobody else was waiting, they took a seat with their drinks.

Shawn pulled one arm across his chest, stretching his shoulder. "That was a good workout. I'll be feeling that tomorrow."

"Yeah, me too." Jude's arms were aching, the good ache of tired muscles, but it might not feel so good the next day. They'd focused on upper body again. Jude had done a legs day during the week, and Shawn had been happy to go with the flow. "What do you do for your thighs?" Jude asked. "You must put some work in there."

"Fuckloads of squats and lunges, mostly. I can do those in my room for free. But I used to do a lot of cycling when I was younger. When I was in the sixth form, I cycled to school and back every day for two years. I think the muscles have a memory, so it doesn't take much to keep them."

"Well, you look good on it, whatever you're doing."

Shawn felt good too. Jude remembered the sensation of those muscular thighs under his hands when he'd sucked him off. They were as hard as iron.

Shawn flushed and smiled. "Cheers."

"Have you got plans later?" Jude asked. "I'm in the mood for vegging out and watching a film. I downloaded *Deadpool* the other day. Have you seen it yet?"

"Yeah, I saw it in the cinema. But I'd watch it again. It's funny."

"Do you fancy that, then? If nobody else is using the TV, we can hook my laptop up to it. Otherwise we can watch it in my room."

"Yeah. Sounds good."

Just then, Jude's phone buzzed in his pocket with a text alert. He got it out and smirked when he saw the message on the screen.

Back in town, fancy a shag?

Sid was a guy Jude had hooked up with a couple of times during the summer. But he'd moved away after graduating, and Jude hadn't expected to hear from him again. Sid was fun and a good fuck. Jude was definitely tempted. He didn't want to sound too desperate, though, given that Sid hadn't bothered to give him any notice.

"Sorry," he said to Shawn. "Just need to reply to this."

Shawn shrugged. "Sure." He got out his own phone while Jude typed his reply to Sid.

Not sure. Pretty busy this weekend, when were u thinking?

Playing hard to get? Sid sent back.

Fuck you.

That's what I'm hoping.

Jude snorted, remembering why he liked Sid. He was an enthusiastic bottom and pushy with it. Getting him to shut up and take it was fun, so he replied.

So, like I said. When were u thinking?

Tonight works for me.

I just made plans for tonight already. Tomorrow?

I'm busy tomorrow. Bummer :(

Jude stared at the screen, cogs turning in his brain. His cock liked the idea of hooking up with Sid. Just the thought of getting to fuck had him sporting a semi. He glanced across the table at Shawn. Cancelling their plans so he could go and get laid would make him a shitty friend, but it wasn't like the movie was more than a casual plan, and Shawn probably wouldn't care. Or maybe they could watch the film and Jude could go and hook up with Sid later.

Shawn looked back questioningly. "Problem?"

"Just getting propositioned and trying to decide whether I can fit him in."

Shawn raised his eyebrows. "Must be nice to be in demand. How many other blokes do you have plans with this weekend?"

His voice had an edge to it. Envy, perhaps? Jude grinned. "It's just this guy I used to hook up with last year. He's back in town and wants to see me, but he's busy tomorrow. I was trying to work out if I've got the energy to see him later after we've watched *Deadpool*."

"Dude, if you'd rather go hook up, we can watch *Deadpool* another time. I don't want to cock-block you."

Shawn's voice was casual—maybe too casual—as he shrugged and looked back down at his phone, and Jude's stomach twisted with something hard to identify. Guilt… or could it be disappointment? Did he *want* Shawn to cock-block him? What the fuck was that about? He frowned at his screen, letting his thumb hover over the keyboard while he hesitated a moment longer before writing *Maybe another time then*.

Decision made, he sent it.

Hope so came Sid's reply. He sounded keen.

Jude wondered if he was back for good or just a visit, but he pushed the thought aside. He had plans with Shawn tonight.

"No. I like the *Deadpool* plan," he told Shawn. "And I need an early night—it's been a busy week. Hooking up is an effort, and my right hand works just fine."

Plus I get to jerk off all over you tomorrow.

Shawn smiled, a genuine smile that made Jude glad he'd turned Sid down. Although the realisation that he'd rather hang out and watch a movie with Shawn than fuck Sid into the mattress was a sobering one… he didn't want to think too hard about what it might mean.

"Your pizza's ready," the guy called from behind the counter, rescuing Jude from his scary train of thought.

Back at the house, they found Jez, Mac, Dev, and Ewan engrossed in a game of *Super Mario Bros*. The guys mumbled greetings but barely glanced up as Jude and Shawn came into the living room, and it certainly didn't look like they were planning on moving anytime soon.

"My room, then?" Jude said.

"Yeah, okay."

"Have fun, lads," Jude said.

"Huh?" Jez looked up briefly with a slightly glazed expression. "Oh yeah, right. Thanks. You too."

"Fancy some beer with the pizza?" Shawn asked. "I've got some in the fridge."

"Yeah that sounds good. Cheers."

They got the beer and headed upstairs.

In Jude's room, they moved the desk over by the bed and set up the laptop on it. As Jude positioned it so they'd have a good view of the screen, it occurred to him what they'd done the last two times they'd set it up like this.

He moved to sit beside Shawn on the bed and wondered whether he was thinking about the other, less innocent things they'd done on the bed together. The credits started rolling and the scents of pizza and garlic permeated the room—probably a good idea to focus on those things instead.

"Let's eat. I'm starving." Jude opened the boxes on the desk and leaned forward to grab a slice.

They soon realised they were going to drop crumbs, melted cheese, and garlic butter everywhere, so they took a box each and put them on their laps, passing slices of pizza and bread back and forth between them.

They ate in silence for a while, engrossed in the movie. When both boxes were empty, they moved the rubbish onto the desk and settled back.

Shawn started licking garlic butter off his fingers. The slurping sound sent Jude's mind to dirty places again.

"Maybe you should go and get more pillows from your room," he said as Shawn tried and failed to make himself comfortable against the wall. "One each isn't really enough."

"Yeah, that's a good idea. Pause this for a minute and I'll go and get them."

"We can wash our hands too. Because you sucking on your fingers like that isn't helping me focus on the film. Just saying."

Shawn flushed and grinned. "Sorry."

Jude licked his own fingers suggestively before leaning forward to click Pause. "You see how distracting it is?"

"Yeah, I get it." Shawn rolled his eyes. "Perv. Okay, I'll be back in a few." He got up and went downstairs.

Jude went and washed his hands in the bathroom. *Calm the fuck down*, he told himself. *Stop thinking about sex and watch the damn film.*

But just the sound of Shawn coming back up the stairs made his heart leap.

CHAPTER NINE

They reconvened on Jude's bed, and Shawn had to agree it was much more comfortable with the extra padding to lean against. Jude also brought a fleece blanket to put over their legs as they were both still in running shorts.

Shawn settled back with a happy sigh. "Yeah, that's much better."

Warm, with a full belly, beer to drink, a good movie, and Jude for company, this was shaping up to be an excellent Friday night.

Shawn was glad Jude had decided to hang out with him. He'd been blindsided by the jolt of jealousy that burned through him earlier when Jude had mentioned who he was texting. What the hell was that about? He had no claim on Jude. Their relationship was a budding friendship at best, so why would he care if Jude was hooking up with another guy?

Pushing those thoughts aside, Shawn tried to focus on the present and stop overthinking.

Their shoulders bumped as he made himself comfortable beside Jude. Shawn didn't try to stop himself from leaning on Jude a little, and Jude didn't seem to care. As Shawn inhaled he could smell their sweat from working out earlier. Not wanting the pizza to get cold, neither had taken the time to shower.

It should be gross, two blokes sitting here together all sweaty from the gym. Yet instead of being disgusting, the mingled scent of their bodies only made Shawn think of other ways they could get sweaty together. That was a dangerous direction to let his thoughts wander in, and he was suddenly glad of the blanket covering his lap.

"We stink," he said lightly.

"Yeah." Jude didn't sound like he minded. "Whatever. I'll shower before bed."

And now Shawn was imagining Jude in the shower, naked and wet. *For fuck's sake.* Why couldn't he get his mind off Jude?

Jude's attention was focused on the screen. "Damn, he's hot as hell," Jude said as Ryan Reynolds was getting down and dirty with the female lead.

Shawn considered this. He'd spent years trying not to consider the relative hotness of male celebrities. He'd often admired them, but had always told himself it was envy rather than fancying them—he wanted to *be* them, not bang them. But now he had to admit that he would totally bang Ryan Reynolds… or wouldn't mind sucking his dick at the very least. The idea of sucking another man off was scary, but thrilling too. He liked what Jude had done to him and was keen to reciprocate, but he wasn't sure how to ask for it—or whether it was wise, especially when his only intimate contact with Jude was on camera. He didn't want to make a twat of himself in front of an audience if he sucked at cocksucking.

Maybe he should talk to Jude and admit that he wanted to experiment off-camera too. But what if Jude didn't want that? Maybe he only wanted Shawn as part of his show, the so-called straight guy to bring in more punters. If Shawn asked Jude for more and he turned him down, it would make things awkward. Shawn didn't want to do anything to derail this tentative new friendship. Since his best mate, Mike, had moved away, he'd been lonely, and now with Beth out of his life too, Shawn needed all the new connections he could find.

"Sorry," Jude said, obviously misinterpreting Shawn's silence as discomfort. "I forgot for a moment there that I wasn't hanging out with one of my mates who's up for ogling hot dudes. Ignore me. The chick's hot too, though. If you're more into that."

Shawn hesitated, gathering his courage. Admitting that Ryan Reynolds was hot seemed like a good first step towards being more honest about himself. "No, it's okay. I was miles away. But actually I think they're both pretty hot."

"Yeah?"

"Yeah." A warm feeling of pride spread through Shawn's chest. He'd done it. He'd admitted out loud that he found men attractive—or one man at least— and the world hadn't stopped turning.

They went back to watching in silence for a while.

Jude broke the silence again. "Am I the first guy you've ever done anything sexual with?"

Shawn tensed, adrenaline pumping through him. He wasn't sure he was ready to talk about that, but Jude was asking, and given the situation between them, he owed him a reply.

"Yeah," he admitted, feeling a weird mix of shame and embarrassment. Was it pathetic that he was so afraid when other guys made it look so easy? It wasn't as though he was short of good role models for men who had sex with other men.

"I'd assumed I was, but I wanted to check." Jude didn't sound as if he was judging him. "Why now, though? I mean… why haven't you done it before?"

Shawn sighed, uncomfortable. "I was resistant to it for a long time. I grew up thinking gay was a bad thing. Everyone at my school used it as an insult, a word you threw around to hurt people. I didn't want that to be me."

"But you're not gay—are you?" Jude asked in surprise. He turned, angling his body towards Shawn.

Shawn met his curious gaze, the movie forgotten. "No." He was very sure about that. "I always liked girls… women. I love being with women. I'm not faking that."

"I never said you were."

"But some people would say I was. That I'm really gay but just scared to admit it."

"Some people are idiots. That doesn't make them right. So you're bi?"

Shawn's heart beat faster. "Yes." He got the word out around the lump in his throat. Just one little word that was so hard to say. But as soon as it was out, he felt lighter somehow. "Yes, I am."

Jude rewarded him with a smile. "Good for you."

Shawn grinned back, floating on the rush of what he'd admitted. *I'm bisexual, and that's okay.*

He still wasn't sure what he wanted. He couldn't imagine telling anyone else yet, but telling Jude still felt huge. And it felt good.

Not knowing what else to say, he turned back to watch the film, letting the warm glow of his admission settle in his chest. Jude's shoulder was warm against his and their bare legs brushed under the blanket. Shawn yearned for more, but he wasn't sure how to make it happen.

For now this was enough. It was good, and he felt happy and hopeful for the first time in ages.

They got drawn into the action of the film, and any interactions between them were focused on that—or on the beauty of Ryan Reynolds's arse in his tight suit.

When the movie ended, Jude moved first, stretching and yawning before closing his laptop. "That was cool. Good film."

"Yeah. It was just as good second time around too." Shawn pushed the blanket off his legs and stood, muscles protesting from sitting still for so long after working out earlier. He lifted his foot up behind him to stretch his quads.

"Sore?" Jude asked.

"Yeah, a little. I'll feel it tomorrow if I don't stretch now."

Jude started gathering up the pizza boxes.

"Let me help you take this stuff down to the kitchen." Shawn picked up the empty beer cans and they went downstairs together.

In the kitchen they found Jez and Mac making toasted sandwiches.

"No, don't put onion in yours or I won't be kissing you tonight," Mac complained.

Jez slapped him on the arse. "I'm sure I can find other uses for your mouth, baby. Oh, hi, guys. Sorry for the TMI."

Jude laughed. "Never TMI. Thanks for the mental image."

Shawn blushed, still uncomfortable with how open Jez was about his sex life. "Whatever, man. I'm totally used to it by now."

"So, what have you guys been up to?" Jez glanced between them.

Jude held up the empty pizza box. "Watching *Deadpool* and eating pizza."

"Awesome. Sounds like the perfect evening—apart from the gym earlier. I'm way too lazy for that shit. Luckily Mac has enough muscles for both of us." He grinned at his boyfriend. "But you two are spending a lot of time together recently. Working out together, movie nights… is this a beautiful new bromance, Shawny? Have you finally moved on after

Mike?" Jez grinned at him, teasing. "Or is there something you're not telling us?"

Shawn felt his hackles rise as anxiety ripped through him. Jez was only teasing, didn't even mean anything by it, but Shawn couldn't help his reaction. Years of denial and overcompensation were hard to shake off. "Don't be a twat," he said roughly. "Can't I hang out with a mate without you reading stuff into it? Not everyone's into dick just because you are."

Years of ingrained habit gave his tone an edge of disgust. As he said it, he glanced at Jude, who looked back. Was that a flash of hurt on Jude's face? That just stoked Shawn's irritation higher. They weren't anything more than friends, so why should Jude care what he said? They weren't even fuck buddies. It didn't count if you were doing it for money. "I need a shower. I'm still gross from the gym." He viciously crushed the beer cans he was holding and shoved them into the recycling bin. "Cheers for the pizza, mate," he said to Jude, not meeting his eye again.

Jude didn't reply.

Shawn stomped upstairs and crashed around angrily as he got out what he needed for his shower.

Once he was under the spray, his irritation receded, soothed away by the steady stream of hot water. Discomfort and a vague sense of guilt crept in to take its place. He sighed as he rinsed suds out of his hair, watching them swirl around the shower tray before disappearing down the plughole.

If only careless words could be swept away so easily. It wasn't that he'd said anything awful, but he knew he'd hurt Jude. Denying even the possibility of anything between them wasn't fair when he'd let Jude suck his dick, hell... he'd begged for it. Ashamed now, he realised what a coward he was. Jude didn't deserve that, whatever their relationship was.

He got out of the shower and dried himself roughly, dragging the towel over his skin like a punishment. He'd apologise to Jude tomorrow.

Shawn was working an early shift on Saturday; he tried knocking on Jude's door when he got home, but there was no reply. When he knocked a second time, Dev's door opened and he peered out.

"Oh," Dev said. "Hi, Shawn. I think Jude's out. He left about half an hour ago."

"Did he say where he was going?"

"Meeting a mate for drinks, I think."

Disappointment was like a punch in Shawn's stomach. He'd hoped to clear the air tonight, but it didn't look like that was going to happen. "Okay, thanks."

Shawn spent a miserable, boring evening alone in his room because he wasn't in the mood to hang out in the living room. Instead he surfed around the web reading articles about bisexuality before getting sidetracked into watching more porn. He tried wanking to some lesbian porn just to check it still did stuff for him—it did, which was reassuring. But somehow, when he came he still ended up thinking about Jude.

On Sunday morning, Shawn woke early and went down to the kitchen to get a glass of orange juice. The house was quiet; all his housemates must still be asleep—if they were even there. Jez and Mac would be, of course, but Dev often slept at Ewan's.

Suddenly he had the uncomfortable thought that maybe Jude had stayed somewhere else last night. He could have hooked up with somcone and not come home. The rush of jealousy that flooded through him at that thought took him by surprise.

What the fuck? He had no claim on Jude; he shouldn't care. But the idea of Jude with another guy made him feel sick to his stomach. Shaking off the pointless thoughts, he decided to go out for a run before breakfast. Maybe fresh air and exercise would shock some sense into him.

After a brisk run along the seafront, Shawn felt a little better. So he made coffee, then got himself a bowl of cereal and took them through to the living room. He turned on the TV, put on a music channel, and watched dancing women gyrating to the beat as he ate.

When he'd finished his breakfast, he took off his running shoes and stretched out on the sofa. He had a day off work today, and it was tempting to go back to bed for a while....

Shawn was trying to decide between a nap and more coffee when he heard someone coming down the stairs. The living room door opened and Jude came in.

"Morning," Shawn said.

"Ugh," Jude grunted.

He was pale and had shadows under his eyes. It didn't make him any less appealing, though. Along with the dark stubble on his jaw and his shaggy mess of hair, it gave him a rakish look.

"Late night?" Shawn asked, trying to sound casual.

Jude yawned. "Yeah, just a bit." He stretched and scratched his stomach, drawing Shawn's attention to the bulge in his sweatpants.

Shawn was desperate to dig for more information about Jude's night, but it was none of his business. "I was about to make more coffee. Do you want some?"

"Oh hell yes… please."

"You look like death warmed up. Have a seat." Shawn got up and gestured to the space he'd left.

Jude collapsed into it and curled up on his side, his hands tucked into the sleeves of his hoodie. Shawn picked up a blanket off the other sofa and chucked it at him.

"Cheers." Jude pulled it over himself.

When Shawn came back five minutes later with two steaming mugs of coffee, he wondered if Jude had fallen asleep. His eyes were closed, a sweep of dark lashes on his pale face. But as Shawn put the mugs down on the coffee table with an audible *clunk*, Jude opened his eyes. "Thanks," he croaked.

"You're welcome." Shawn took a seat on the end of the sofa by Jude's feet.

Maybe now was a good time to apologise. Jude looked too tired to still be annoyed with him, and Shawn had just brought him caffeine, so… "I'm sorry about Friday night."

"What?" Jude seemed to wake up a little at that, frowning and rolling onto his back so he could prop his head on the armrest and meet Shawn's gaze.

"When Jez was taking the piss about us hanging out together. I… I don't know. I didn't handle it very well, and what I said wasn't cool."

"Oh, yeah." Recognition dawned and that hurt was there again.

Shawn felt shitty for reminding him about it. The temptation to duck away from Jude's intense gaze was strong, but he forced himself to hold it. "I'm sorry if I made you feel bad."

Jude sighed. "It wasn't a big deal. I get that you aren't ready to come out to anyone else yet, and Jez kinda put you on the spot when you weren't prepared." He paused. "But it did hurt a bit, not gonna lie. I mean… I know we're just fooling around for the webcam, and it doesn't mean anything, but this is why I usually try not to get involved with blokes who are in the closet. It never feels good to be denied, especially when you made it sound like there was something *wrong* with liking dick. You really need to stop doing that."

"Yeah. Fuck." Shawn felt like a right wanker, but he knew he deserved it. "I'll try not to do it again."

"Old habits are hard to break." Jude's face softened a fraction. He kicked Shawn's thigh with his socked foot. "But you'll learn."

Shawn grabbed his ankle. "Cut it out." But he relaxed, relieved to be forgiven.

Jude cleared his throat. "Speaking of liking dick, you still up for this evening's show? It's no skin off my nose if you want to give it a miss because it's messing with your head and making stuff too complicated for you."

"No!" Shawn replied immediately, only realising how much he'd been looking forward to it when Jude casually threatened to pull the plug. "No, I want to."

A pleased smile spread over Jude's face. "Okay, cool."

Shawn flushed, glad that Jude seemed happy that he wanted to carry on with their arrangement. He squeezed Jude's ankle where his fingers were still wrapped around it, then let go.

They drank their coffee, watching TV in silence. A little later, Shawn glanced back at Jude and saw he'd fallen asleep. Smiling, Shawn turned the TV off and crept out without waking him.

CHAPTER TEN

"Fuck's sake, you lazy bastard. Did you even make it to bed last night?"

Jude got a rude awakening when Jez threw himself down onto the sofa by his feet, bouncing and making Jude's stomach lurch. He hadn't drunk loads last night, but enough to feel rough.

He rubbed his eyes as Mac sat on the floor in front of him. Jez had turned on the X-box and was powering it up for *Call of Duty*; the display told Jude it was around midday.

"I did make it to bed. This is a nap. Or it was till you fuckers ruined it for me."

"Aw." Mac turned and ruffled Jude's hair. "Sorry, mate. But duty calls—ha! See what I did there?"

Jez and Jude groaned in unison.

"So, what did you do last night?" Jez asked.

"Met some mates for drinks, then went to the Palace. Stayed there really late."

"Did you hook up?"

"Nah."

Jude had thought about it. There'd been lots of hot blokes on the dance floor, and a few had tried their luck with him, but he wasn't feeling it. Instead he kept imagining what it would be like to dance with Shawn and how he would react to being on a dance floor surrounded by shirtless queer guys. Would he love it? Or would it send him running back to his closet?

Fucking Shawn... even though Jude had been pissed off with him for his stupid comment on

Friday, he still hadn't been able to stop thinking about him. At least Shawn had apologised now.

Jude ran his tongue around the inside of his mouth. He was thirsty, and his mouth tasted gross. "Ugh, I feel disgusting. I need fluid, food, and fresh air. Preferably in that order. See you later, guys."

He heaved himself up off the sofa and left Jez and Mac to their game.

After rehydrating and eating a huge plate of cheesy oven chips and baked beans, Jude got some fresh air and exercise by walking the long way round to the supermarket to stock up on food for the week. He carried his heavy bags home, and then hit the shower after unpacking them.

He spent the first part of his afternoon online, doing some research. He wanted to ask Shawn whether he'd be up for being restrained, but Jude hadn't really done that other than with his ex using a tie, and with one bloke he'd hooked up with once who had all sorts of fancy leather cuffs and rope and stuff. Jude didn't have anything like that, but he'd be able to improvise with something. The Internet proved very helpful in that regard.

The research made Jude horny, but he resisted the urge to jerk off, so he'd have a better load for the cam show later. A bit of anticipation always made it more fun for him too.

He caught up with Shawn in the kitchen at teatime, but as Dev and Ewan were in there too, it wasn't the time to broach the subject. Instead, Jude greeted them all with a hi.

"Alright," Ewan said.

Dev turned and nodded from where he was stirring something on the hob. "Hi, Jude."

"Hey. You look better than you did earlier. Did you have a good nap?" Shawn's smile softened his features.

Jude couldn't help staring for a moment. Shawn seemed softer somehow, less guarded than he'd always been before. Jude wondered if he was the only one who got to see this side of Shawn. The idea gave him a thrill of satisfaction. "Yes, thanks." He flushed. "I wasn't that hungover, really. I was just out late."

He went to his cupboard and got out some bread to make a sandwich. Shawn already had the toasted sandwich maker heating up while he sliced cheese.

"Are you having two rounds, or have you got space for mine in there too?" Jude asked.

"You can put yours in. We can always make more after."

Shawn was having ham and cheese; Jude went with cheese and tomato.

Once their sandwiches were ready, they took them through to the living room. Nobody else was in there, so they sat on the sofa with their plates on their laps.

Shawn turned the TV on and flicked through a few channels till he found some football. "This okay?"

"Sure." Jude was moderately interested in football, and the players were always worth ogling even if he wasn't following the match.

He wasn't able to follow the game today, though, because his mind kept turning over images of Shawn naked and tied to a chair.

Fuck. Jude squirmed, getting hard at the thought of it. He was going to be really disappointed if Shawn didn't want to play. Maybe it was better to find out sooner rather than later. They were alone, so there was no time like the present…

"So, I was wondering if you wanted to try something different today?" He angled himself so he could see Shawn.

Shawn side-eyed him, his mouth full of toasted sandwich. "Mmm?" He raised his eyebrows.

"How about you let me restrain you while I do stuff to you? When I teased you about being tied up, a lot of the commenters seemed to like the idea."

And so did you. He didn't say that part out loud.

Shawn's eyes bulged and he seemed to have trouble swallowing his mouthful of sandwich. That shouldn't have been sexy, but Jude's brain was apparently locked onto a twenty-four-hour internal porn channel right then, because it only made him think about other things Shawn could choke on.

When Shawn finally swallowed, he cleared his throat; his cheeks flushed pink as he said, "Yeah. Okay. I mean… if you think it would earn us more tips."

"Oh yeah. Definitely." Jude played along. He was pretty sure now that Shawn wasn't only in this for the money. But if he needed to pretend that money was the motivating factor, then Jude wasn't going to ruin it for him.

"Yeah, well, that's fine, then." Shawn chuckled nervously. "I'll try anything once."

"Come up half an hour before we're due to start and we can work out exactly what we're going to do."

"Okay."

Jude went back to his room to google for a final check on the restraint method he was planning on trying with Shawn, as long as Shawn was okay with it. He watched the demonstration video and tested it out a few times to make sure he had it down. After that, he tidied his room ready for filming—the piles of dirty clothes in the corner would look a bit shit. Anticipation built as he waited for Shawn to show.

When a knock sounded on the door, Jude's heart spiked with nerves as much as excitement. "Come in."

Shawn looked as anxious as Jude felt, and Jude wondered whether they were doing the right thing by trying something new so soon, especially with an audience. What if Shawn didn't like it but didn't feel he could say anything while the camera was rolling?

Shawn closed the door and locked it, then stood with his hands in his pockets and his body tense.

"Are you okay?" Jude wanted to go over to Shawn and reassure him physically. He instinctively knew Shawn would respond to his touch, but would it be weird?

Shawn gave a curt nod, but a muscle ticked in his jaw.

Fuck it. Jude crossed the room and put his hands on Shawn's shoulders. Shawn's eyes flew wide, but he didn't flinch; he held Jude's gaze, chin up and eyes steady.

"Are you sure you want to do this?" Jude asked. "It's totally your call. If you've had second thoughts, it's fine."

"I want to," Shawn said quietly.

Jude searched his face for uncertainty, but he didn't find it. He moved a hand to the nape of Shawn's neck and squeezed. "Good. I do too." Shawn relaxed, letting out a slow breath as his shoulders dropped. "But we need some ground rules. I need to know what you're okay with, and what you're not, and we need a signal for me to stop if it becomes too much."

"What, like, if I'm going to come?"

"No. I mean for me to stop if you don't like something or if you freak out and want to stop the scene."

"Like a safeword?" Shawn's brow furrowed.

"Yeah, exactly. Have you ever used one before?"

Shawn shook his head. "No. I've never done anything like this before. Well… not this way round. One of my exes got me to use handcuffs on her once, but I've never been on the receiving end." He licked his lips nervously.

"Traffic lights are what a lot of people use. Green for go ahead, yellow for slow down or pause, and red for stop."

"That sounds easy to remember. Let's go with that."

"Okay. So red means we stop completely, I untie you, and we turn off the camera. Yellow just means a bit of time out, but don't use it for warning me you're close to coming. Just tell me if that's the problem. It's hotter that way." His cheeks heated at the thought of it, and Shawn's eyes darkened.

"Yeah?" Shawn said hoarsely.

"Yes." Jude loved it when Shawn was right on the edge and he had that absolute power over him. There was nothing sexier than having a guy right on the brink of orgasm, and he got to decide whether to let him come or not.

He still had his hand curled around Shawn's nape. The skin was warm and damp, and Jude wasn't sure whose sweat it was—maybe a little of both. He had the heat turned up high in his room, ready for getting Shawn naked later. Needing to break the tension a little, he drew away and gestured to the bed. "Sit down there for a minute while I finish setting up."

Instead of moving the desk to its usual place for filming, Jude set up his desk chair in the space by the bed. His laptop was on the desk by the wall, and he turned it on and opened the webcam, making sure the chair was in full view. He picked up a pillow and placed it on the floor in front of the chair.

Glancing back, he saw Shawn watching curiously. "For my knees," he explained. "You're going to be in the chair."

Shawn's cheeks reddened and he swallowed, throat bobbing. "Okay."

"I'm going to use a pillowcase to tie your wrists together. Is that all right with you?" Shawn nodded. "We still need to discuss what you're happy for me to do. I assume stuff we've already done is fair game? Hand job? Oral?"

Shawn nodded again, his flush even deeper. Jude was gratified to see a significant bulge in the front of his sweatpants now. "What about anal play? Is that something you'd be into?"

"I… I'm not sure."

It wasn't a no. Encouraged, Jude pressed a little more. "I could use my fingers, or a dildo."

"Not your dildo. It's too big—I've never done that before. But maybe your fingers."

Jude narrowed his eyes as everything suddenly became clear. "How do you know how big my dildo is?" His suspicions were confirmed by the reddening of Shawn's face, but he wanted Shawn to admit it.

Shawn stared at him wide-eyed, his mouth slack with horror and his face now the colour of a beetroot. "I, uh…."

"Shawn?"

Shawn covered his face with his hands. "Fuck, this is embarrassing. But I, um. I watched you, okay? After the time when I walked in on you and realised what you were doing. I saw the logo of the website and looked you up. I wanted to—I don't know. See for myself, to be sure."

"And you watched it all?"

Shawn nodded, still hiding his face. "Yeah. I'm sorry. I know it was really creepy, but I couldn't help myself."

Jude moved and sat beside him. He took Shawn's wrists and pulled his hands away so he could see his expression. He looked ashamed, afraid of what Jude might say to him. "Hey," he said softly. "It's okay. I don't mind."

"You don't?" Surprise replaced some of Shawn's guilt.

"No. I can see why you'd be curious. And it's not creepy when I'm putting myself out there for the world to watch. You didn't do anything wrong."

"I suppose." Shawn still looked doubtful.

"And you know what else? I think it's fucking hot that you watched." Jude squeezed Shawn's wrists where he was still holding them. "Did you jerk off while you watched me fuck myself?"

Shawn nodded. "Yeah." His voice was barely more than a croak.

"Did you wish it was your dick in my hole?"

Shawn stared at Jude as though mesmerised by his words. "No… I…." He took a shaky breath. "I thought about how it must feel for you. I… touched myself there, with my fingers."

A jolt of heat seared through Jude like a lightning bolt. His cock ached, rock-hard from the conversation. "Fuck."

"I'd never done that before, or let anyone else— but it made me come." The confession spilled from Shawn's lips as if he'd been holding it in and the dam had burst. "When I touched my—my hole, it made me come so fucking hard."

"You're killing me." Jude realised he was gripping Shawn's wrists so tight it must be painful. He loosened his grip and rubbed his thumbs apologetically over the skin. "Jesus Christ, Shawn. The thought of that. Fuck." He shook his head, trying to make the fog of arousal clear, and glanced at the clock by the bed. Five minutes to go. Back to business. "So, can I use my fingers on you today?" He needed to be sure, but *God*, he wanted to after what Shawn had just said. He wanted to show Shawn how fucking amazing it could feel to have someone finger you, someone who knew what they were doing. He wanted to light Shawn up like nobody ever had before, to make him come harder than he'd ever come in his life.

"Yes," Shawn said. "I want to try it."

"Awesome." Jude broke the tension by giving him a blinding grin, which Shawn answered with a tentative smile.

Jude was knocked sideways by a sudden urge to kiss him, which he tamped down immediately. Shawn wasn't his to kiss. That wasn't what this was, but Jude felt a wave of longing, wishing that things were different between them.

For now, though, he had to focus on the present. He had a job to do.

"It's nearly time to start. Take off your hoodie and socks and sit in the chair. Have you got underwear on today?"

"No," Shawn said.

"Good, that's one less layer to strip you out of. I was going to keep most of my clothes on this time, if that's all right with you? It helps set up the dynamic for the scene, I reckon, with you naked and me fully clothed."

"Okay." Shawn's cheeks were still flushed and his dick was still hard. He was obviously okay with that idea.

"Cool."

Jude busied himself on Twitter for the last couple of minutes before it was time to begin. He tweeted the link to the show, announcing it was about to start, and replied to a few fans who were waiting impatiently.

"Right. You ready to roll?" he asked. Shawn nodded. "Then have a seat." Jude gestured to the chair and Shawn sat with his hands on his thighs, rubbing the fabric nervously. "Don't forget. Yellow means pause, red means stop."

"Okay." Shawn huffed out a breath.

"Let's go." Jude clicked on the record button.

And they were live.

CHAPTER ELEVEN

Shawn tried to relax. His body was taut as a guitar string; the merest touch would make him vibrate with sensation, humming with pleasure.

Jude sat on the edge of the bed, leaning in so the webcam could see him. "Hi there, folks." He smiled.

Shawn wondered how he could look so relaxed. Surely he had to be feeling nervous too, even if only a little.

Messages began to pour into the chat box, greeting them and making the usual comments about how hot they were, or asking to see their dicks or their arses—even their feet. There was always someone asking for a close-up of feet.

"I have something extra special for you today," Jude said to the camera. "Some of you might have noticed that Chris here likes it when I take charge. Well, today he said I can tie him up and have my wicked way with him. So that's exactly what we're going to do a little later. But first, he's looking a little tense, so I'm going to loosen him up with a massage while you guys get tipping us."

With that, Jude got up and moved to stand behind Shawn. Shawn watched the screen. Jude's face was no longer visible, but most of his torso was. He put his hands on Shawn's shoulders, a heavy weight as he pressed down and squeezed. Shawn let out a breath and forced his muscles to give under Jude's touch.

"You're all knotted up," Jude rubbed and pressed through the thin fabric of Shawn's T-shirt, seeming to know exactly where Shawn was holding his tension.

"This would be easier without your shirt on, though. Can I take it off?"

"Yeah." Shawn's voice cracked a little. "Okay," he added more clearly.

"Arms up."

The casual command in Jude's tone did things to Shawn and he obeyed immediately, already relaxing as he followed the order. It was so good to let Jude take charge and make the decisions. Shawn liked doing as he was told. Life was so much less stressful with someone else in the driving seat.

The cooler air that hit his skin as Jude drew his shirt up and off made Shawn's nipples tingle and tighten immediately.

"That's better." Jude's hands were back, touching his skin now, warm and sure where they caressed him. He kneaded at the meat of Shawn's shoulders, pressing his thumbs firmly into the muscle in a way that made Shawn want to groan, or maybe purr like a cat. It felt so good. He let his head fall forward, giving in to the wonderful sensation of being looked after. "Is that okay?"

"Yeah, it's amazing," Shawn answered honestly. "So good."

Jude kept going, squeezing a little harder.

Shawn grunted, but it was a grunt of pleasure, not pain. He lost himself for a while, closing his eyes and just feeling. His thoughts drifted away, and he barely noticed when Jude's touch changed gear, becoming gentler and more sensual. But when Jude smoothed his hands down over Shawn's collarbones to his chest, he abruptly came back into the moment. His nipples hardened again as Jude skimmed them with his palms, and he sucked in a breath, cock jumping in his sweats.

"You like that?" Jude's voice was low and sexy as hell.

"Yes."

Jude slid his hands up Shawn's neck to tousle his hair, scratching deliciously at his scalp. Shawn made a noise that was somewhere between a moan and a whimper.

"Yeah, that's hot," Jude murmured. Then he added more loudly, as though wanting to make sure the mic picked it up, "You're turning me on with those little sounds you make. Reminds me of how you sound when I suck your dick."

Jude moved closer, and Shawn could feel the hardness of his erection against his shoulder. Shawn moaned again, shifting in his seat. Without thinking about what he was doing, he put a hand on his cock and squeezed himself through his clothing.

"Oh no you don't," Jude said immediately, pulling Shawn's arm back and pinning it behind him. "That's mine."

Just like that, all Shawn's tension was back, but in a good way. It crackled like static, making his skin tingle and his dick throb. Jude's grip on his wrist was tight and punishing and perfect. "Please," he said hoarsely.

"Please what?" Jude's voice was silky-smooth. "Tell me what you want me to do to you."

Shawn swallowed, aware they were being watched by hundreds of strangers. He felt wanton, desperate, with an edge of shame about being so needy. But the shame acted like tinder to the flames of his arousal. "Tie me up so I can't touch myself. Then do it for me. Touch my cock. Get me off."

"Fuck yeah. Yeah, okay."

Jude moved around into Shawn's line of vision, erection tenting his sweats and his face flushed; he was clearly as into this as Shawn was. Shawn felt relief at that, and pride, glad that Jude wanted him as much as he wanted Jude. His gaze snagged on Jude's bulge and his mouth flooded with saliva as he imagined taking it in his mouth. He wanted it, badly, but he wasn't brave enough to ask for it. He didn't want a camera running for his first time sucking another guy's dick.

Jude picked up a plain white pillowcase from his desk and moved around behind Shawn again. Speaking to the camera he said, "I don't own any cuffs or rope, and I didn't have time to buy any, so we're improvising today." Behind Shawn's back fabric rustled. "Give me your hands."

Obediently, Shawn put both arms behind the back of the chair and Jude slid two loops of material over them. Jude made an adjustment that drew the loops tight, tying Shawn's wrists together firmly. "How does that feel?"

Shawn tested the binding. It was snug. He couldn't work his hands free, but it was still comfortable. He could probably stand and lift his arms over the chair back if he wanted to get away, but he wasn't going to—he was happy where he was. Having his wrists tied just meant he couldn't touch himself no matter how impatient he got or how much Jude teased him. That realisation gave him a thrill. Jude was in charge and Shawn had to take whatever Jude gave him. "Feels good."

Jude moved around to stand in front of him again. "You okay?" His expression was serious. Shawn nodded. "Sure you want to do this?"

Shawn nodded again. "Yeah," he managed. His throat was dry with anticipation.

"Okay, remember. Red if you want to stop." Jude nudged his legs apart and then dropped to his knees between them.

He started by stroking Shawn's chest and stomach. Jude's hands were warm and left delicious tingles of sensation as he focused on Shawn's nipples with his fingertips, teasing them back to hardness again. He pinched them lightly and Shawn jerked; his hands held by the fabric hit the back of the chair. The reminder that he was bound and helpless made his cock ache. He was already painfully hard, wet and sticky against the inside of his sweatpants, and Jude hadn't even touched him there yet.

Jude pinched again, a little harder, rolling Shawn's nipples between his thumbs and forefingers and watching his reactions carefully. Shawn sucked in a sharp breath, unsure whether he liked the pain. It was hard to decide.

Jude seemed to pick up on his uncertainty and moved in closer, warm breath caressing Shawn's chest before his tongue made contact.

Shawn definitely liked that. A moan escaped his lips as Jude licked and sucked on a nipple, his mouth hot and wet. Shawn's cock flexed against fabric, as though yearning to be stroked or sucked.

As if Jude could read his mind, he gradually moved lower. Not as fast as Shawn would have liked, but definitely going in the right direction. His tongue tickled and the slight stubble on his chin scratched as he licked and kissed his way down Shawn's abs until he reached the bulge in his sweatpants. He licked over the material, open-mouthed, driving Shawn crazy as his warm breath seeped through the fabric. It was so close to what he needed, but not nearly enough.

"Ju—" Shawn caught himself just in time, remembering he couldn't use Jude's name. "Come *on.*" His voice came out sounding whiny, but he was too far gone to feel embarrassed about that.

Jude flicked his gaze up to meet Shawn's and gave him a mischievous grin. "Getting a bit desperate there, *Chris?*" He emphasised Shawn's pseudonym.

"You know I am," Shawn gasped. "Come on. Suck me."

Seeming to take pity on him, Jude reached for the waistband of Shawn's sweats and eased them down. Shawn's dick sprang free as Jude tucked the fabric below his balls, pushing them up. The air was cool against his overheated skin and his cock jerked, eager for Jude's mouth. Precome beaded at the tip and spilled over.

Jude licked his lips. "Look at you. Fuck, you're so hard."

"Yeah. So are you going to do something about it, or what?" Irritation flared and Shawn's tone did nothing to hide it.

Jude smirked. "Ask me nicely."

Shawn growled in frustration. "Please!" It still came out sounding pissy, though. He tried again. "Please, suck my cock."

Those seemed to be the magic words, because fucking *finally* Jude lowered his head; his shit-eating grin vanished as he parted his lips and sucked Shawn's cock into his mouth.

"Fuck," Shawn hissed, his toes curling with pleasure. He was wound so tight already. If Jude went hard and fast, he'd come embarrassingly quickly.

Jude must have realised that because he paced it perfectly with long, slow strokes in an uneven rhythm. Between bouts of cocksucking, he pulled off and licked Shawn's balls or pressed ticklish kisses to his stomach, making him curse and writhe in the chair because it felt good but wasn't what he needed.

Shawn lost track of time as Jude worked him over. It could have been five minutes, ten, or twenty. It was impossible to tell when he was a twitching mess of desire, his body tight with the need to come.

Jude focused his attention on Shawn, ignoring whatever was going on in chat. Shawn almost forgot they had an audience, and it wasn't until Jude stopped what he was doing completely that he opened his eyes, saw himself on the laptop screen, and remembered they were doing this for show. He was flushed right down from his cheeks to his chest, and his ribcage lifted with every breath.

"Don't stop!" Shawn strained against the ties on his wrists, lifting his hips and tensing his muscles.

"I think it's time to try something new." Jude tugged on the waistband of Shawn's sweats. "Lift up."

Shawn raised himself just enough that Jude could slide them down and off.

Jude put his hands on Shawn's thighs and pushed them a little farther apart; then he gripped Shawn's hips and pulled so his arse was resting on the edge of the chair. "That's better." Jude put his forefinger in his mouth and sucked it until it was wet and shiny.

Shawn's heart surged, panicky and desperate as he realised what Jude was about to do.

"Can I?" Jude held his gaze, his expression serious once more.

Shawn nodded. His voice cracked as he replied. "Yeah. Do it."

Jude stroked Shawn's cock with his other hand as he slid the wet finger back behind Shawn's balls to rub over his hole. Shawn was so sensitive there; nerve endings lit up as Jude circled his finger and Shawn gasped. Pinned between the grip of Jude's hand on his dick and the pressure of his finger below, he had nowhere to go.

"Relax. Let me in." Jude's voice was calm and sure.

Shawn's body responded without him making a conscious decision. His tight muscles gave and the tip of Jude's finger slipped inside, strange and wonderful all at once. He squirmed, squeezing around it and gasping at the weird feeling.

"You okay?" Jude just let his finger sit there. He didn't try and move it or push in deeper; his other hand was still on Shawn's cock, stroking him, grounding him, keeping him hard.

"Yeah," Shawn managed breathlessly. He wanted something, wanted more… but he wasn't sure he could take it. He felt so tight around that one finger.

Jude moved, withdrawing a fraction, then pushing in deeper. Shawn hissed and tensed. It burned a little and he wasn't sure he liked it, but as Jude did it again and then again, it felt better each time. Shawn bore down, his body begging for more.

But instead of giving him what he wanted, Jude pulled his finger free. He chuckled at Shawn's whimper of protest and patted his leg. "I'm just getting the lube. That'll make it even better."

And he was right. If Shawn thought one spit-slick finger was good, it was nothing compared to the sensation of Jude pushing back in with two slippery fingers. The extra tightness and pressure made him gasp and panic for a moment—it was almost too much. But then Jude curled them and brushed against a place inside him that made Shawn's whole body light up.

It was different to anything he'd ever felt. Heat pooled inside him, urgent and imperative as Jude kept rubbing carefully over that spot. *Holy shit.* So this was what all the fuss was about! No wonder guys liked anal; it felt fucking incredible. Jude wasn't even touching Shawn's cock now, and that was a bloody good thing, because he suspected that if Jude so much as breathed on it, it would be game over.

"You like that?" Jude asked, his smug smile telling Shawn that he was well aware how much he liked it. Jude just wanted him to say it for the camera, or maybe for himself.

"Fuck *yes*," Shawn managed, not caring how desperate and breathy he sounded. "It's amazing. Don't stop!"

His orgasm was building, a wave gathering strength and momentum, poised ready to break and crash over him. But without stimulation to his cock, he couldn't quite get there. He moaned in frustration, pulling his bound arms futilely against the back of the chair. "I want to come." It sounded almost like a sob. "Please."

But Jude, damn him, slowed the movement of his fingers and ran his other hand over the straining muscles of Shawn's abs, carefully avoiding his erection, which was red and angry—pretty much like the rest of Shawn.

"Soon," Jude said. "We're just going to keep this going a little longer because you look so fucking fine like this. I think the guys are enjoying it as much as I am, seeing you tied up and begging so nicely."

Jude was so calm, so in control. For a moment, Shawn wondered whether he was affected by this at all. He couldn't see Jude's bulge with him down on his knees, still fully dressed, but his cheeks were flushed, his pupils dark. He must be turned on—Shawn hoped he was. He hoped Jude's cock was aching as much as his own.

Jude dipped his head and Shawn's heart leapt, hoping he was going to suck him off again and finally let him come. But instead, Jude nuzzled his balls, breathing in deeply and murmuring, "So fucking hot, Jesus."

Jude's fingers inside Shawn were still now, so Shawn squeezed around them, moving his hips as much as he could, trying to fuck himself on them. Jude snapped his head back up, amusement on his face along with a hunger that gave Shawn hope. Jude moved in close, his words barely a whisper so there was no way the camera would pick them up. "God, you're such a little slut for this. I bet you'd love it if I bent you over and stuck my cock in you, wouldn't you? Would you let me do that, Shawn? I think you would. I think you'd beg me for it."

The sound of Jude saying his name made Shawn hot all over. His words were so dirty, but so true. Shawn didn't even feel ashamed for wanting that, not any more. "Yeah," he whispered back. Not for the camera, not for show. All for Jude. "Yeah, I'd let you fuck me." He tightened his muscles again, clamping around Jude's fingers, and this time it was Jude who groaned.

Jude drew back so Shawn could see his face, and Shawn's desperation was reflected back at him. And Shawn begged. "Make me come. Please."

Jude nodded. Then he dipped his head and sucked Shawn's cock into the slippery heat of his mouth. He sucked and swirled his tongue as he started to fuck Shawn with his fingers again, hard and fast and perfect.

"Oh fuck, yes." Shawn jerked against his bindings again, his whole body straining tight. "J—I… I'm there!"

He started to come in Jude's mouth, but Jude pulled off in time for the second spurt to paint a stripe up Shawn's stomach. Jude's lips were wet and parted, with come on them, and Jude licked it off as he stroked Shawn through his orgasm, teasing out every last drop until he was twitching with oversensitivity.

Only then did Jude take his hands off Shawn and stand. "I need to come too." His voice was tight and desperate. He moved to stand by Shawn's shoulder, shoving his sweatpants down and gripping his cock where it jutted out, rock-hard and eager. He angled his body so he'd be on camera as he started to stroke.

Shawn couldn't tear his gaze away, watching as the slick head emerged from Jude's fist. When he breathed in he could smell it, musk and sex, and he *needed...*

"Come on me." The words broke free without his conscious permission. "Come on my face."

"Fuck." Jude gasped, a strangled sound, and he barely had time to point his cock at Shawn before he came. Thick, warm splashes hit Shawn's face and he closed his eyes instinctively, even though he wished he could see. Jude groaned, and then Shawn felt the gentle touch of Jude's fingers on his lips. He opened his eyes and met Jude's gaze.

Jude looked as overwhelmed as Shawn was. They stared at each other, and Shawn wanted to say something, to tell Jude how he felt. This wasn't about money; it wasn't about experimentation any more. He didn't know what it was, but it was huge and scary and important.

Then Jude seemed to pull himself together. "Well, that was hot as fuck, don't you think, guys?" He turned to the webcam and wiped his hands on his shirt before pulling his sweatpants back up. "I think Chris enjoyed it too."

Shawn could hear tension in Jude's voice, and he seemed to be rushing to finish as he did his usual spiel, thanking people for watching and for the tips, and finally reminding them about his next show.

Shawn suddenly panicked. Still tied to the chair, naked and exposed, he wanted to cover himself but couldn't. Something cracked open and his heart pounded, his breathing became unsteady. He bit his lip, trying to control himself as he waited for Jude to hit Stop.

As soon as Jude closed the lid of the laptop, Shawn gasped out, "Untie me!"

Jude wheeled around, concern on his face. "Sorry, sorry. Of course." He hurried around behind the chair and crouched down to release Shawn's hands.

As soon as he was free, Shawn grabbed his sweats and pulled them on. His hands were shaking and he shivered, suddenly cold where before he'd been hot. His skin broke out in goosebumps.

"Here." Jude handed him his T-shirt.

Shawn pulled it on hurriedly, smearing the come he'd forgotten was on his face. He stood, wanting to escape. He needed his bed, somewhere safe and warm where he could collect his scattered thoughts and regain his equilibrium. He swayed, suddenly dizzy.

What the fuck is wrong with me?

"Hey." Jude put his hands on Shawn's shoulders and pushed him back down into the chair. "Give yourself a minute. That was intense. It's not unusual to feel pretty shaky after a scene like that. You went pretty deep there for a while."

His words didn't make any sense, but Shawn couldn't be bothered to ask him to explain.

"I'll just get you a cloth, you're a mess. Don't move. Just breathe. In… out… in… out. Slowly."

Having some instructions to follow was reassuring, so Shawn stayed put and focused on pulling air into his lungs and letting it out. He was dimly aware of the click of the door as Jude left the room and then the sound of water running in the bathroom. Then Jude was back with a warm flannel. He knelt beside Shawn and wiped his face gently.

He came on my face. Because I asked him to. Shawn had the sudden urge to laugh hysterically. He bit it back, making a weird snorting sound instead, and shivered again.

"Are you cold?"

"Yeah. No. I don't know."

Jude stood and pulled back the duvet on the bed, then came back and took Shawn's hands, pulling him up. "Come here." He guided Shawn to the bed. "Lie down."

Shawn didn't have the energy to argue. Jude sounded determined, and Shawn wasn't sure he wanted to be alone when he felt so weird and light-headed, disconnected from his body.

Jude got into bed with him and pulled the covers up, then wrapped his arms around him. Shawn let Jude tug him close until his head was resting on Jude's chest. The thump of his heart was reassuring, a steady beat that gave Shawn something to focus on as his heart rate slowed.

In pieces, he became aware of physical sensations again. His body warmed and the shivering stopped; his breathing levelled out. Jude's arms were tight around him, grounding him, but he still felt as though he might float away if Jude released him.

He didn't want Jude to let go.

After what felt like a long time, Jude spoke, his voice soft. "You feeling better now?" His breath ruffled Shawn's hair.

"Yeah." Relaxed now, Shawn realised he was exhausted. Wiped out by whatever weird reaction he'd had earlier. "I should probably go. Otherwise I'm gonna fall asleep here."

But he didn't move, and nor did Jude.

"You don't have to. In fact I'd rather you stayed so I can keep an eye on you."

"What, in case I have another funny turn?" Shawn tried to make it sound like a joke, but his cheeks heated. He was embarrassed at how he'd freaked out earlier. "I'm fine now. I don't need a babysitter." He wriggled out of Jude's embrace to lie on his side next to him where he could see his face. "I don't know what happened before, but I'm okay."

"It's a thing that sometimes happens. I read about it online. Something to do with your endorphins crashing back down."

"What, after sex?" Shawn frowned.

"Well, yeah... but especially after the sort of thing we did. Bondage, BDSM, whatever you want to call it. It's more intense than regular sex sometimes."

Shawn didn't know what to say to that. He could hardly deny it. Jude had blown his mind tonight. *Intense* seemed woefully inadequate to describe how he'd felt, how he'd lost himself in the act of... *submitting* to Jude. "I suppose. But you still don't need to look after me. I'm fine now."

Jude's face did something complicated. "Maybe I *want* to look after you."

His voice came out gruff. He reached out tentatively and cupped Shawn's cheek, and Shawn's heart surged. Of all the ways that Jude had touched him, nothing had gone right to his core the way that simple caress did. "Stay for a while longer."

"Okay," Shawn said simply.

Jude smiled and then moved closer and pressed a soft kiss to Shawn's lips. It wasn't a sexual kiss; it was achingly sweet and made Shawn long for things he couldn't articulate, even to himself. He closed his eyes as Jude put his arms around him again, wrapping one arm over Jude's torso, and snuggled close. It was weird being cuddled by someone so big and strong, but it was definitely good-weird.

As Shawn let himself drift into sleep, his last conscious thought was that he could get used to this.

CHAPTER TWELVE

Jude's thoughts whirled while Shawn slept.

He kept replaying what had happened. It had been the most erotic experience of his life, and it was weird to think that it had been shared by a myriad of faceless strangers. During the show his focus had all been on Shawn. He'd barely been thinking about the people watching. Shawn had been all that mattered.

At the end he'd fucked up, though. What had he been thinking leaving Shawn tied up and naked? Talking to the webcam instead of checking in on him and making sure he was okay? Shawn might have had a weird reaction after the scene anyway, but Jude blamed himself for being slow to realise what was going on. Not that he was an expert in such things, but he'd read enough online to know that sub drop was a thing, and that as the dominant one in their "relationship"—for want of a better word—he should have planned things better in terms of aftercare. He wouldn't make that mistake again.

If I haven't scared him off and he wants to do anything like that again.

Jude sighed, breathing in the scent of Shawn's hair. Hope and uncertainty were an ache in his chest. Fooling around with Shawn on camera was supposed to be fun, uncomplicated, no-strings sex to help boost his income, while letting Shawn work out whatever he was trying to work out about himself. But now, with Shawn in his bed and all these feelings he could no longer deny, Jude realised he'd got himself into a situation he hadn't anticipated, and he was yearning for things that seemed impossible.

Jude had to admit that he really liked Shawn. After spending time together and doing the things they'd done, he more than *liked* him. If this was straightforward—no pun intended—and Shawn was out of the closet and ready to date a guy, then Jude would ask him out. Ask him if he wanted a relationship, something exclusive. Because Jude thought it could work if Shawn wanted it too. They got on well, and they were clearly sexually compatible. The chemistry between them was off the charts, and Jude knew Shawn felt that too; there was no way he could be faking his reactions.

But he's not out.

And there was the problem. Because although Shawn had admitted he was bi to Jude, Jude was pretty sure nobody else in Shawn's life had a clue. And given how threatened Shawn had been when Jez had so much as hinted at something between them the other day, it was safe to assume that Shawn wasn't ready to come skipping out of the closet to be Jude's boyfriend.

Just then, Shawn stirred, breaking Jude's train of gloomy thoughts. He made a sleepy *mmph* sound and lifted his head, blinking in the light from the bedside lamp.

"Hey, sleepyhead," Jude said quietly.

"What time's-it?" Shawn slurred.

Jude craned his head to see the clock. Shawn could have seen it himself if he looked, but his eyes were barely focused. "Half eleven."

"Ugh. I don't want to move, but I need a piss."

Jude didn't want Shawn to move either. He wasn't sure whether it was protectiveness or possessiveness, but he didn't want to let Shawn out of his sight. "It's only next door," he said lightly. "I'm sure you can make it."

"I ought to go and get ready for bed and then try to get back to sleep." Shawn stretched and yawned, seeming a little more awake now. "I've got an early shift tomorrow. I should leave you in peace anyway. I'm sorry about earlier." He avoided Jude's gaze. "I feel like an idiot."

"It was my fault. I should have been more careful."

Shawn shook his head, his face sceptical. "Whatever. Let's just forget about it." He pushed himself up and climbed over Jude to get out of the bed.

Jude had the feeling that something was slipping away from him—something important. He was worried that if he let this moment of intimacy pass he'd never get it back. He sat up and grabbed Shawn's wrist, saying quickly, "Will you come back and sleep in here tonight? You freaked me out a little earlier, and I wanna keep an eye on you."

"I'm fine now."

"Maybe, but will you anyway? Please?" The memory of Shawn saying *please* to him earlier flashed into his head.

Make me come. Please.

Now it was Jude's turn to be vulnerable, to be honest about what he wanted. He wasn't ready to lay it all out there, but he could ask Shawn to spend the night with him.

Shawn studied him, his brow slightly furrowed. Whatever he saw on Jude's face must have convinced him, because he gave a curt nod. "Okay."

Jude relaxed, trying to hold back a smile. "Good. See you in a few, then."

While Shawn went downstairs to do what he needed on the floor below, Jude used the top floor bathroom between his room and Dev's. He brushed his teeth and rinsed, then stared at his reflection in the mirror for a moment. He ran a hand through his dark curls and frowned. What was he doing? The way he felt about Shawn was scary. There was so much potential for heartbreak when Shawn wasn't on the same page. But the wheels were already in motion; Jude was on this ride whether he wanted it or not, and it was too late to get off. He had to hang on and see where it took him.

Back in his room, Jude kept his T-shirt on but decided he'd be too hot sleeping in sweatpants. Still commando from earlier, he dropped his sweats and was about to step into some boxers when his door opened again.

"Oh, sorry." Shawn stood there looking flustered, his face red as he turned away to shut the door. He was dressed in just a T-shirt and boxers, ready for sleep.

Jude chuckled. "You've seen it all before, mate."

But he pulled his underwear up quickly. Everything felt different between them now. Their cam sex sessions had been structured, negotiated in advance. But this? This was new territory, and Jude felt out of his depth. "You can turn around now."

Shawn turned with a sheepish smile. "I should have knocked."

"Story of your life." Jude gave a nervous chuckle.

They stared at each other for a moment.

"So… uh. What do you want to do?" Jude asked. It was like an awkward sleepover. As the host, Jude felt he needed to keep Shawn entertained. "Are you ready to sleep again, or do you want to watch something on my laptop? I've got Netflix."

"Are you suggesting Netflix and chilling?" Shawn gave him a cheeky grin.

"No!" It was Jude's turn to blush. "I mean... I would, but I didn't think...."

There was another long pause, and Shawn's grin melted away to be replaced by uncertainty—maybe a hint of wistfulness? Hard to tell, but there was something there that gave Jude hope and the courage to blurt out, "Do you want to? Fool around off-camera, I mean? Because I wouldn't say no if that's something you want to try."

Shawn's eyes widened and darkened, and his gaze flickered down to Jude's lips. He looked nervous and horny all at once, and apparently that was a combination that really worked for Jude, because it sent a spike of want through him that had his heart pounding and his dick getting hard.

Please say yes. Please say yes. Please say yes.

"Okay." It sounded like the word was forced out through a dry throat. Shawn swallowed. He still looked terrified, like an animal about to flee.

Jude realised that if this was going to happen, he had to take charge. Shawn was never going to make the first move. That was okay. Jude could do this. He liked being in control. Shawn liked him being in control.

He moved forward slowly, right into Shawn's space until their toes were nearly touching. Standing this close, Shawn had to look up at him. Shawn was physically more powerful, but Jude had a couple of inches on him in height. He wondered how that felt to Shawn, to be looking up at someone who was about to kiss him.

He took Shawn's face in his hands and held his gaze, giving him a final chance to pull away. Finally he leaned in and pressed his lips to Shawn's.

At first Shawn was frozen, his lips soft but unresponsive, arms limp by his side. But then Jude kissed him again, parting his lips and using his tongue lightly as though asking Shawn for permission. It was as though he'd unlocked something, because Shawn melted into him, opening his mouth and becoming an active participant. He put his hands on Jude's hips and pulled him closer, giving as good as he got as they explored each other's mouths.

Arousal built slowly but steadily, ramping higher with each touch of Shawn's tongue, each rasp of their stubbled chins. When Shawn slid his hands down and gripped Jude's arse, tugging him close, Jude felt Shawn's erection against his own and moaned into the kiss.

He moved his hands down to Shawn's waist, sliding them up the back of his T-shirt he stroked over the smooth, warm skin. Shawn's muscles shifted as he squeezed Jude's arse more tightly.

Wanting more, Jude broke the kiss and tugged on Shawn's T-shirt. "Can I?"

Shawn answered with a smile and lifted his arms up. Jude drew the T-shirt over his head and then stripped out of his own. Shawn's gaze dropped to Jude's chest, and his eyes were hot and hungry. He ran a tentative hand over the sprinkling of dark hair there and then brought it up to curl around the back of Jude's neck, guiding him down for another kiss.

Desire made Jude's legs weak as more blood rushed to his dick. He didn't want to rush Shawn, but suddenly being horizontal was a necessity. He broke away from Shawn's lips, gasping as he latched onto his neck instead and sucked. *Fuck*. He was so enthusiastic.

"Bed?" Jude managed.

Shawn grunted something that sounded like agreement, but he seemed reluctant to stop kissing Jude even for the few seconds it would take them to relocate. So Jude took charge, grabbing Shawn's arms and wheeling them around so he could push Shawn back towards the bed. Shawn was probably stronger than he was and could have resisted, but he didn't. He let Jude manhandle him, shoving him down onto the mattress. Jude straddled him, much as he had in the cam show, and pinned his hands above his head. This time it wasn't for an invisible audience. It was real and raw, and he could see in Shawn's eyes how much he wanted this—wanted Jude to take control.

Shawn lay still, watching him, his only movement the lift of his ribs with every harsh breath.

Jude's heart pounded as the tension stretched out between them, elastic reaching its breaking point.

"What do you want?" he asked, needing to be absolutely sure that everything was on Shawn's terms. "I need to know. Do you want me to hold you down? I'll do whatever you like, but it has to come from you."

"I want…." Shawn looked up at him, holding his gaze as he licked his lips. His eyes were wide, and Jude could tell he was nervous. Then Shawn's gaze dropped to the bulge in Jude's boxers and his eyes darkened, desire obvious on his features. "I want to suck your cock," he finally said in a rush. "I've never done it before, though—obviously." He flushed. "So I'll probably be crap at it. But I want to try."

Fuck, Shawn's eagerness and the fact that this was a first for him pushed all Jude's buttons. He was afraid he wouldn't last long when he got his dick in Shawn's mouth. But maybe that wasn't a bad thing if it was Shawn's first time.

"We can do that." Jude lowered himself over Shawn, rubbing their hard-ons together. "But first I want to kiss you again."

He took Shawn's mouth in a slow, sensual kiss, losing himself in the wet slide and warmth of it. Shawn kissed him back, letting Jude hold his arms where they were. He ground up against Jude's hips, though, seeking friction, and as their cocks brushed, he moaned into the kiss, a needy sound that drove Jude to move things along.

He sat back on his heels, and once again Shawn's gaze tracked down to Jude's cock where it strained against the fabric of the grey boxer briefs he was wearing, a dark patch of precome at the tip. Jude pushed his boxers down a little so he could get his dick out. He stroked himself, showing off and loving the way Shawn watched so intently. He looked so hungry for it.

"You want it?"

"Yes." No hesitation.

"How do you want to do it? Me on my back? Sitting on the bed so you can kneel on the floor? Tell me what you want, Shawn." The grip of his hand on his cock was almost too much. Jude held himself around the base, squeezing tight so the veins bulged.

"I want it like this. Me lying down."

Jude hesitated. Appealing though that mental image was, he wasn't sure that was the best way to break in a cocksucking virgin. "Are you sure? It might be easier if you have more control than that."

Shawn gave a small shake of his head. "I don't want to be in control. I want you to put it in my mouth. Make me take it."

"Holy shit, Shawn." Jude's cock was aching now, clearly on board with that plan. "I'm going to have to stick it in your mouth to stop you saying shit like that, otherwise I'm in danger of coming all over you before we even get started."

Shawn gave a huff of laughter, but still kept his gaze fixed on Jude's dick. "Do it, then." He flexed his arms where they were still pinned, as if he wanted to reach for Jude.

Okay. Jude felt like he'd given Shawn fair warning. He'd just have to be careful not to get carried away.

Jude went up into a plank position so he could get his boxers off completely and kick them away. Then he took Shawn's off too before straddling him again. He knee-walked up the bed. "Pull that second pillow down a bit. That'll make the angle better."

Shawn propped his head up higher and lay waiting. His arms were still over his head even though Jude wasn't holding them there any more.

"Perfect." Jude grinned. Taking his cock in hand, he rubbed the tip along Shawn's lower lip, leaving a glistening smear of precome.

Shawn opened his mouth, licking at Jude's cockhead. He made a small sound of desperation.

"God, you want this so badly, don't you?" Jude said in wonder. "Okay, baby. You can have it." He angled his hips forwards and pushed into the wet, slippery warmth of Shawn's mouth.

Jesus. Not getting carried away was easier said than done. The expression on Shawn's face was one of bliss as he took Jude in and sucked. It was obvious that he was no expert, but Jude wasn't a perfectionist. As long as teeth weren't involved, it was hard to go too far wrong with a blow job, and sloppy could be hot too—especially with someone so obviously desperate for his cock as Shawn was.

Bracing himself on one hand, Jude thrust gently, forcing himself to keep it slow. With his other hand, he touched Shawn's face and stroked his jaw, feeling the muscles working as he sucked. Some spit leaked out of the corner of Shawn's mouth and Jude caught it with his thumb, smearing it along the stretch of his lip.

"You look so fucking hot," Jude muttered. "So good. Taking my cock like this."

Shawn's gaze flicked up to meet Jude's and held.

"Are you okay?" Jude wanted to check in.

Shawn made a muffled affirmative sound, put his hands on Jude's hips, and urged him to go faster.

"You're gonna make me come," Jude warned him breathlessly, fucking into that wet, perfect heat. The threat of orgasm pooled in his balls, a wave gathering strength.

Shawn seemed okay with that, squeezing his fingers into the meat of Jude's arse. He gagged a little, throat closing tight around the head of Jude's cock. Jude tried to pull away, but Shawn kept him there, eyes watering as he adjusted to the feeling.

Then Jude couldn't hold back any more—the pressure of Shawn's throat, the sight of him letting Jude *use* him like this was too much. "Fuck, I'm coming."

His cock pulsed and he emptied his load.

Shawn choked again but still gripped Jude's arse tight, not letting him go. Jude cried out as Shawn swallowed around him, the squeezing sensation almost too much.

Finally, Shawn relaxed his hands and Jude withdrew his softening cock. Even then Shawn chased it, catching it in his hand and licking the last few drops from the tip as Jude hissed, oversensitive. Shattered, sated, and overwhelmed by the whole experience, he flopped onto the mattress beside Shawn. He tugged Shawn towards him and kissed him. He couldn't find any words, but he could show Shawn his gratitude this way.

As Shawn turned onto his side, his erection was obvious against Jude's hip. Jude was relieved to feel the physical proof that Shawn had enjoyed what they did as much as Jude had. Well… maybe not quite as much, because he hadn't come yet. But that was easily remedied. Jude reached down and curled his hand around Shawn's cock, finding it gratifyingly wet and slippery.

He stroked and Shawn moaned, thrusting into his grip. They were still kissing, deep, passionate kisses with an edge of desperation. Carried along on the tide of Shawn's desire, Jude's cock was still half-hard, and when Shawn came with a groan, slicking Jude's fist, Jude could almost feel Shawn's relief as if it were his own.

Their kisses slowed now, became gentle, achingly sweet. With Shawn's cock softening in his hand, Jude didn't want the moment to end. Something had changed between them, the boundaries had shifted, and they needed to talk about this thing, too obvious and too shattering to ignore. But even as Shawn clung to Jude and kissed him like a parched man drinking water, a kernel of anxiety niggled away in Jude's chest.

It's too good to be true. Life is never this easy.

It was Shawn who finally pulled away, but only far enough to settle his head on the pillow and grin goofily at him. "That was amazing."

"Yeah?" Jude smiled back.

They were sticky with come, but neither seemed keen to move. Jude wiped his hand on the sheet and then settled his palm on Shawn's hip, wanting to keep the physical contact.

Shawn's brow furrowed and he bit his lip. Jude could tell he was working up the courage to say something. He tried not to get his hopes up.

"Thank you," Shawn said finally, in a rush of something that sounded like relief.

"What for?" Jude was genuinely confused. "I should be the one thanking you after that."

"For letting me do what I did… for making me feel good about wanting the things I do." His face flushed a little but he carried on, determined. "It's something I always wanted—not so much the doing-stuff-with-a-guy part—but playing like that, letting someone dominate me, take control."

"Couldn't you have tried it with a girl?"

"Maybe if I'd met the right one? But Beth was more the other way, to be honest. She wanted to be the one tied up and taken care of. And with hook-ups or casual relationships, I never trusted anyone enough to tell them what I wanted."

Jude wondered what that made them, if not a hook-up or a casual relationship, but he wasn't ready to ask. Not tonight. He didn't want to derail Shawn from this rare moment of honesty. But they needed to talk about it soon. After tonight, Jude wanted more than casual. "Well, I'm glad you trust me."

"You knew anyway." Shawn said with a smile. "You could tell the first time you grabbed my wrists and joked about tying me up. I gave myself away."

"You weren't hard to read. But I think maybe I was attuned to it because I like doing stuff like that in bed too."

"Do you always like being the dominant one?"

"I've tried both ways, and I can enjoy either role." Shawn looked worried, so Jude hurried to reassure him. "But I prefer it this way."

Shawn relaxed. "Oh, okay. Cool. I mean… I wouldn't want to think you weren't into it."

"Shawn." Jude squeezed his hip. "In case you couldn't tell—but if you couldn't, then you need your eyes tested or your head read—I was definitely into it."

Shawn chuckled. "Good to know."

Shawn yawned, and Jude noticed the dark shadows under his eyes—he looked exhausted. It was past midnight now, and it had been an intense evening. "We should sleep," Jude said.

"Yeah," Shawn agreed. "I'm all sticky, but I'll shower in the morning. Can you set an alarm? I'm working at eight, so you'll need to set it for half six. Sorry. That is, if you're still sure you want me to stay?"

"Yes." Jude reached over Shawn for his phone on the bedside table. He unlocked it and set an alarm with a few taps, then put it under the pillow. "There. I'll wake you when it goes off. Can you turn the lamp off?"

Shawn rolled away to hit the switch, and Jude admired the stretch of muscle in his shoulders before he disappeared into darkness. Then there was the creaking of bedsprings as Shawn made himself comfortable. Wanting contact, Jude shuffled closer, and when he reached for Shawn, he found he was on his side, facing away. Jude spooned in behind him, putting a hand on Shawn's waist. "Is this okay?"

"Yeah." Shawn took his hand and pulled it up to his chest. Lacing their fingers together, he held it there. "Yeah. 'S good." He sounded half-asleep already.

Jude smiled against the back of his neck and listened to Shawn's soft breathing until sleep pulled him under too.

CHAPTER THIRTEEN

Shawn was woken by an unfamiliar sound. An alarm, but not his, and muffled... sounding faraway.

He stirred and realised there was a heavy weight across his chest—an arm—and a knee poking his thigh.

Jude.

And the noise was presumably Jude's alarm that he'd set for Shawn last night, promising to wake him.

Shawn snorted. Jude was dead to the world and completely oblivious. Shawn moved carefully, trying not to jolt him awake, and slid a hand under the pillow to grab Jude's phone.

The increase in volume as he pulled it out made Jude grunt and startle. "Mmph. Wha—?"

"It's okay, just your alarm going," Shawn said as he swiped to stop it. "Go back to sleep."

"Ugh. Too early."

"Yep." The last thing Shawn wanted to do was get up for work. But needs must. He heaved himself up and out of their warm cocoon, and then he stumbled around in the darkness of Jude's room, trying to find his clothes. They'd slept naked, which Shawn now realised was bad planning as he failed to locate his underwear and T-shirt from wherever Jude had flung them last night.

Suddenly the lamp by the bed clicked on, flooding the room with dim yellow light. Shawn straightened up quickly, resisting the urge to cover himself. It was a bit late for modesty. "Thanks." He cast around the room. "There they are." He grabbed his boxers and stepped into them quickly. Feeling marginally more comfortable with his parts covered, he found his T-shirt in a heap by the bed and put that on too. Jude's sleepy gaze on him made Shawn's skin prickle with uncomfortable heat.

His brain suddenly supplied Shawn with the memory of Jude kneeling over him last night, his cock in Shawn's mouth. A wave of arousal flooded through him, followed by a lurch of anxiety.

Everything felt different this morning.

Last night, carried along on the high of what they'd done together, it had felt okay. Shawn had been totally driven by pleasure and the freedom of finally giving in to his desires, he hadn't had time to worry about what any of it meant. Even after, when they'd gone to sleep together, he'd felt safe and content. But now, wide awake in the chill air outside Jude's bed, everything came into focus a little too sharply.

He'd revealed himself to Jude in a way he never had with anyone—his bisexuality, his kinks, things he was barely comfortable with himself were out in the open between them. But who was Jude to him? They were friends, housemates, but that was all. Was Shawn stupid to have trusted him with this? What if Jude told someone, bragged about it with Jez and Mac, joked about what Shawn was into?

Surely he wouldn't… but Shawn couldn't stop his worries from spiralling out of control.

"I'd better go," he said quickly, anxious to escape to the shower and wash away the evidence of the night before.

"Okay." Jude sat up in bed, the covers pooling around his waist. His voice was still rough with sleep. "Have a good day."

Shawn swallowed. He stared at Jude for a moment, a rabbit caught in headlights. He should probably give him a hug or a kiss or something. It seemed wrong leaving without offering that, at least. But he bottled it and turned for the door instead. "See you later."

"Yeah, see you."

Was that disappointment in Jude's tone?

Then Jude added, "We should probably talk tonight."

Shawn's stomach lurched. He looked over his shoulder and met Jude's unreadable gaze. "Yeah," he managed. "Yeah. Probably."

Hurrying out of Jude's room, he literally walked right into Dev, who was coming out of the bathroom on a waft of toothpaste and shower-steamy air. "Shit!" Shawn jumped out of his skin. He hadn't been expecting to see anyone else at this time of the morning. Nobody else in the house started work or lectures as early as him.

"Oh, sorry!" Dev clutched his towel, gaze taking in Shawn's boxers and T-shirt. With his hair all mussed from sleep, it must be obvious where he had spent the night. Shawn saw the realisation dawn on Dev's features, eyes widening and jaw dropping. It would have been almost comical if Shawn hadn't been busy freaking out.

Dev said, "I, um, didn't know you and Jude…."

"We're not!" Shawn snapped quickly. "It's not…. We were just watching a film together, and I fell asleep."

Because obviously mates watch movies in their underwear together, in bed. Fuck's sake.

Dev looked about as convinced as the explanation warranted. "Whatever, Shawn. It's none of my business. And it's not like I care who you… watch films with." His lips curved in something that approached a smile, but he quickly wiped it away, obviously sensing Shawn's tension. "Don't worry about it. If it makes you feel better, I never saw you."

"Thanks." With that, Shawn escaped down the stairs to the middle floor, his heart pounding in his ears and his palms sweating.

He wasn't sure if Dev's assurance of secrecy *did* make him feel better. Now he felt kind of shitty for trying to deny it, because how homophobic was that? It was insulting to Jude, and by extension to Dev, and he was letting himself down by not being honest. But it was a lot to deal with when he was still figuring things out, and he knew he wasn't ready to be open about what was happening between him and Jude.

Hell, we haven't even talked about it ourselves yet.

After a hot shower, a speedy breakfast, and a chilly walk to work, Shawn's thoughts were still a jumbled mess. He was distracted, making stupid mistakes on the till. His line manager took him off the till and sent him to unpack new stock onto the shelves instead. That was a more soothing activity than trying to deal with customers, but it only gave Shawn more time to think.

If this was just about sex and experimentation, it would be easier if he didn't *like* Jude. He'd only gone into this to work out his attraction to guys. It wasn't supposed to have turned into anything. But as he and Jude had got closer, they'd become friends, and it was hard to separate the sex from the rest of it.

When it was on camera, there had been a distance between them, some of the time, at least. Shawn had caught glimpses of what Jude would be like as a lover rather than a showman. But last night had stripped away all pretence. Everything they'd done together last night had been because they wanted it. Because they wanted each other. And for Shawn, that went beyond sex. Falling asleep with Jude's arms around him had felt so terrifyingly *right*.

What did that mean for him? Experimenting with his bisexuality was one thing. Hooking up with guys, having some casual sex while he was young and carefree. But when it came down to it, Shawn had still supposed he'd end up with a woman. Sure, guys could marry guys in this country now—and that was great. For all his bitching about PDAs with Jez and Mac, he was happy they'd have that option if they wanted it one day. But that was never something Shawn had imagined for himself. When he thought about his future, it was always with a woman, and kids who were conceived without the help of a surrogate.

Now Jude had turned all those assumptions on their head.

Not that Shawn wanted to *marry* him. That was more than a little premature. But the way he felt about him? He knew it could turn into something serious if Jude felt the same way, and if Shawn was brave enough to try, and what did that mean for his future? If he wanted to be in a relationship with Jude, he couldn't hide it, like he'd tried to do that morning. He felt a spike of shame at the memory. Jude was out and proud. He wouldn't want to be dragged back into the closet by Shawn, no matter how much they liked each other and how hot the sex was.

Ugh.

Shawn shoved bottles of shampoo onto the shelf too hard and some of the ones at the back fell over. He muttered a curse and got side-eyed by a bloke a little farther down the aisle.

"Sorry," he said.

"Bad day?" The man grinned sympathetically.

"Yeah. Not the best."

"Hope it improves, mate."
"Cheers. Me too."
But it didn't.

By the time Shawn got home, he hadn't come any closer to working out what he wanted to say to Jude. He had no clue what Jude wanted from him anyway. Maybe Jude would want to keep it casual. That might be for the best, even though Shawn wasn't sure how easy that would be after last night.

He should have been starving after a long day at work. He'd had a sandwich at lunchtime, but that was all. When he got home, he went straight to the kitchen out of habit, but his gut felt uneasy with nerves and tension. He couldn't be bothered to cook anyway, but he ought to eat something, so he made a couple of slices of toast and jam and took them up to his room. He ate them while he changed out of his work clothes and into his usual sweats and hoodie.

Once he'd eaten, Shawn thought he'd better wait for Jude to come to him. He tried to play a game on his laptop for a while, but he couldn't focus on it, too keyed up and nervous about the conversation they needed to have. So he decided to man up and go and see whether Jude was in his room.

He tapped lightly on Jude's door; his heart pounded as he waited.

"Come in," Jude called. "Oh, it's you. I was thinking about coming to find you." He gave Shawn a smile, but it was a shadow of his normal grin. Jude looked as anxious as Shawn felt.

"Hi." Shawn shut the door behind him.

Jude sprawled on his bed, sitting up against the pillows with textbooks and notes spread around him. Shawn took the desk chair and tried not to think about the last time he'd sat in it—but it was impossible. A sense memory gripped him, of Jude's fingers inside him while he strained against the chair. His body flushed hot and longing swept through him. It was more than just arousal. Jude *got* him. He'd known what Shawn needed, and he'd taken care of him. Nobody had ever made Shawn feel like that before.

"So, um. How was your day?" he asked, fidgeting with the cuff of his hoodie.

"Come on, Shawn. Let's skip the small talk and cut to the chase," Jude said with a half-hearted smile. "I don't know about you, but I don't want to waste time talking about our days when we need to talk about what happened last night."

Shawn shrugged, wary of showing his hand. "I don't know what to say. Stuff happened. It was good."

"Do you want to do it again? Like that, I mean. No camera. Just us."

"Yes." No hesitation. That part was easy to admit to. "Do you?"

"Hell yes." Jude's face was serious now. "But—" He took a deep breath. "—if we're gonna carry on doing that, I need to know if you can be in a relationship with me. Because I don't just want you to be a fuck buddy. But I'm not sure you're ready for more, even if you care about me." Hurt crept over his features. "I heard you talking to Dev this morning on the landing—the doors in this place are pretty thin. And if we're going to carry on doing this, then I don't want it to be something you're ashamed of. That would suck."

Shawn's face burned. Guilt flooded him at the thought of Jude overhearing that conversation. "I'm sorry. I just freaked out and didn't know what to tell him. He didn't believe me anyway."

"Yeah, but that's not the point. Your first instinct was to lie about it. And I understand why. You're new to all this, and only just coming out of denial. But I care about you too much to go along with that. I can't be your guilty secret, Shawn. That would make me feel like crap, and I'd end up resenting you for making me feel bad."

"So, what are you saying?" Shawn was struggling to process Jude's words. It was all too much too soon. "Is it all or nothing? You want to be with me, but only if I come out and tell everyone?" The thought of that made his stomach turn over and defensiveness made his temper flare. "Because I don't think it's fair to push me to come out before I'm ready."

Jude shrugged. "Maybe it isn't. But I'm trying to protect myself. I know what I need if I'm going to be in a relationship with someone. I need to be with a guy who isn't ashamed to be seen with me. I'm not prepared to hide away like a criminal. I'm proud of who I am."

Jude stared at him, with determination on his face, but hope too.

Fuck. Shawn wished so much that he could feel the same. He envied Jude his certainty and his confidence. But the idea of telling all his friends and his family that he was in a relationship with a man seemed impossible. He was torn, his heart pulling him in one direction while his fear pulled him in another.

There was a long pause, before finally Shawn spoke around the lump in his throat. "I don't know if I can do that. Not yet, anyway." His chest ached, and the blatant disappointment on Jude's face was like a lance to Shawn's guts. "I'm sorry," he added huskily.

"But you do like me?" Jude asked then. "Not that it helps, really. Maybe it will only make it worse to know…. But if it wasn't for me wanting to be open about things, would you want to be with me? In a relationship, not just for sex?"

"Yes." Shawn's voice cracked and his eyes prickled dangerously. He figured Jude deserved this honesty, even if it hurt more to know what he was throwing away because of his cowardice. "Yes. I really like you. I've never felt like this about anyone before. But it's too soon for me to come out. I'm not ready for that yet."

"Fuck." Jude gave a harsh chuckle that sounded nothing like amusement. "Yeah, okay, that does actually make it worse. I almost wish I hadn't asked."

"I'm sorry," Shawn said again, helplessly. He could see his misery reflected back on Jude's face. "So… where do we go from here? Do you still want to do the shows together?"

He felt a pathetic surge of hope. If Jude said yes, then at least Shawn would get to keep that contact with him.

"I don't know. I think it would mess with my head, and maybe yours too. We crossed a line last night. That meant a lot to me, and I think it did to you too." He watched Shawn carefully with narrowed eyes.

Shawn couldn't deny it; the tug in his heart was the proof. "Yeah. Yeah it did."

"So I'm not sure I can go back to messing around on camera with you. Not now feelings are involved, it would be too weird and depressing."

"That's it, then," Shawn said. "It's over?"

"I guess." Jude shrugged sadly. "I think it's for the best."

"Can we still be friends?"

Shawn regretted the words as soon as they were out. Not because he didn't mean them—he didn't want to lose Jude's friendship—but because he sounded so needy and pathetic. But he did want Jude in his life, in whatever form that took. He'd hate it if he lost Jude completely.

"Sure, I guess. I mean... you won't be coming out to any gay bars as my wingman, but we can still go to the gym together and hang out here." The corner of Jude's mouth lifted in an encouraging smile.

The thought of Jude out in gay bars doing God knows what to wipe Shawn from his memory made his stomach lurch with jealousy, but he squashed it down. He didn't have the right to feel that way when he was the reason things couldn't work between them. He had to let Jude get on with his life. "Cool," he managed. "Okay, well... I'd better go and leave you to get on with your work." He gestured awkwardly at the books and papers. "Good night, then. I'll, uh, see you around."

"Sure. Night, Shawn."

Shawn left without looking back. But when he closed the door behind him, his throat was tight and hot and his eyes prickled with unshed tears. A wave of emotion crashed over him, anger as much as sadness. He headed down the stairs to his room. Blinking back tears, he barged into his room and slammed the door behind himself. "Fuck, fuck, *fuck*," he swore at the empty room.

After throwing himself down on the bed, Shawn punched his pillow a few times. His mum had taught him to do that when he was a little kid with a short fuse. Taking out his aggression on an innocent pillow was preferable to hitting his older brother. When his arm started to ache, he lay on his back with his pillow hugged tight against his chest and glared at the ceiling.

He was furious with himself for not having the balls to do what Jude asked of him. But he was also furious with Jude for putting him on the spot and making him choose. Would it have killed him to have cut Shawn a little slack? Given him a little time to work through things before demanding that he came out?

Shawn wasn't even sure what was holding him back. His family would probably be okay. Shocked maybe, but they weren't the sort to disown him or be really shitty about it. Some of his old mates would take the piss, but they could fuck off. If Shawn did decide to tell people, he knew he'd be able to weather the storm.

But it was up to him to choose when. He resented the way Jude had made it sound like an ultimatum. All or nothing. Now or never.

Ugh.

He pulled the pillow over his face and sighed.

CHAPTER FOURTEEN

Jude stared at the back of his bedroom door after Shawn's exit.

Well, that was a fucking disaster.

He flopped back on his pillows and ran his hands through his hair, tugging on the curls so hard it hurt.

Maybe he shouldn't have said anything. By pushing for more too soon, he'd fucked it all up. But damn, it had made him feel crap when he'd heard Shawn talking to Dev and denying everything between them. He couldn't handle that. And how would it work anyway if they tried to keep it secret? His housemates weren't stupid. Dev was already suspicious. They'd get caught out eventually if they tried to sneak around behind the guys' backs. It was better to have it out in the open.

Except now there was nothing to be open about. Perhaps if he'd given Shawn more time, things would have been different.

"Fucking idiot," he muttered, not entirely sure whether he was referring to himself or Shawn.

Maybe it applied to both of them.

Jude was amazed at how easy it was to avoid each other for the next few days. Not that he was consciously trying to stay out of Shawn's way, but as he was feeling pretty miserable about everything, he preferred hanging out in his room alone rather than dragging everyone down with his shitty mood.

When Jez and Mac tried to get him to play video games with them, he claimed assignment deadlines, which wasn't a complete lie, and stayed in his room putting some half-hearted effort into his uni work, in between playing games online as a distraction.

On Wednesday night he did his cam show at the usual time. He didn't say anything on Twitter beforehand, other than the usual announcement to remind his fans. But as soon as he was live, the questions started pinging into chat.

Where's ur mate?
No Chris tonight?
What happened to your str8 friend?

"Yeah, I'm afraid Chris can't make it today." That was all the explanation he gave.

The questions kept coming.
Why?
Sorry mate. Did he find a new girl?
Will he be back?

Jude ignored them. "Sorry, guys, but I'm afraid you'll have to make do with me solo again. But I've got my dildo for company, so if you're feeling generous, you might get to see some arse-fucking action later."

That distracted most of them.

Jude got on with the show, trying hard to stay focused on putting on a good performance.

But everything he did reminded him of Shawn. It was lonely doing this on his own. He'd rather it was Shawn's hand on his cock, or him bringing Shawn off for the camera—or without the camera. The exhibitionism of performing had been undeniably hot, but the connection they'd had when nobody was watching was even better.

As Jude edged himself closer to climax, fucking himself with his dildo and stroking his cock painfully slowly, he remembered teasing Shawn the last time they'd done stuff with an audience. He thought about how Shawn had loved Jude's fingers in him, how he'd begged to come.

I'd let you fuck me.

Jude closed his eyes and imagined Shawn on his hands and knees, taking Jude's cock, and that was what finally tipped him over the edge into a gasping, shuddering orgasm—a few minutes sooner than he'd intended.

"Fucking hell," he gasped, so lost in his fantasy that he'd almost forgotten he was on camera. "That was intense."

Nice load
That was hot
What were you thinking about?
Were you thinking about Chris?

It was only then that Jude wondered whether Shawn might be watching. Was it weird that he hoped he was?

"Yeah. I was thinking about him," he said. "I was imagining fucking his tight arse and showing him how much he'd like it."

It was Shawn's loss that he'd never find that out now.

Jude finished up his show a little early. The usual emptiness descended when he cut the webcam, and it was worse than it had ever been before. He had a quick shower to clean up and then went on Netflix to find something funny to watch, hoping to distract himself from the heavy weight of loneliness that sat on his shoulders. But even his laughter at *Arrested Development* felt hollow and did nothing to lift his mood.

When he went to bed, it took ages for him to fall asleep even though he was tired. His thoughts kept circling back to Shawn and were full of regret and disappointment.

Shawn knew he shouldn't have watched Jude's show tonight. He felt guilty. It seemed even more of a violation now to allow himself to get turned on watching Jude, to jerk off to him wanking on-screen, when he wasn't prepared to admit his feelings for him to anyone else. But he hadn't been able to stop himself. Like an addict, desperate for a fix, it had been all he'd been able to think about as the time for Jude's show crept closer.

Watching him going through the motions, it was obvious to Shawn that Jude's heart wasn't in it. He wondered whether the other watchers could tell too? Sure, he put on a good show. He teased them and got himself hard, but there was an emptiness to his expression; the spark of fun was missing.

It wasn't until Jude got close to orgasm that he seemed to truly lose himself in the act. Shawn was jerking off too as he watched, waiting for Jude to come before he'd let himself join him. Jude squeezed his eyes shut when he came, shaking and gasping as he held the dildo deep inside himself, coating his hand with come. "Fucking hell. That was intense." His voice was rough.

Still stroking his dick, close now, his focus entirely on Jude, Shawn wasn't paying attention to the comments. Jude opened his eyes and focused on the screen. His lips twisted in an unhappy smile.

"Yeah. I was thinking about him." Shawn didn't need to check to know Jude was talking about him. "I was imagining fucking his tight arse and showing him how much he'd like it."

"Fuck." That mental image was all it took. Shawn came, thinking about that and exactly how much he wanted it.

Once the high of orgasm receded, Shawn felt lonely, guilty, and miserable.

He lay awake for hours, considering a possible future where he and Jude were together, thinking about how he'd handle coming out, and all the people he'd have to explain himself to.

Then anxiety came to join the mess of emotions clamouring for attention in his heart and head.

He couldn't do it. Could he?

On Friday night, in an attempt to be sociable, Shawn emerged from his room. Hiding away had meant he didn't have to deal with seeing Jude, but he missed the company of his other housemates.

Jez had noticed Shawn was quieter than usual; he was annoyingly perceptive like that. When he badgered Shawn to come down and play *Mario Kart* with him and Mac on Friday night, Shawn had agreed.

What Shawn didn't know was that Jude was also part of this plan. He suspected Jude wasn't aware that Shawn had been invited either, because there was a moment of awkwardness when he went into the living room to find Jez, Mac, and Jude on the sofa waiting for him. He paused for a beat longer than was socially acceptable.

"Hey, Shawny." Jez's tone was as casual as always. "Hurry up and join us, it's all lined up ready to go."

Of course, the only space on the sofa was next to Jude. Shawn met his gaze as he walked across the room.

"Hi." Jude's smile was a little forced.

"Hey." Shawn sat down.

With four of them on the sofa, there wasn't a lot of personal space, but this was the best sofa for being able to see the TV screen. Shawn tried not to touch Jude, but it was impossible. Their shoulders bumped and so did their knees as Shawn made himself comfortable.

"Here." Mac passed a controller to Shawn.

"Cheers."

"Okay, ready?"

It was a relief when the game started and gave him something to focus on other than the warmth of Jude beside him.

They played a few rounds, and then during the final race of a set of three, Jude's phone chimed, then chimed again.

When the race was over Jude got his phone out to read the messages.

Shawn resisted the urge to look over his shoulder as he tapped out a reply.

Another message came back immediately and Jude chuckled.

"Come on, Jude," Mac complained. "Stop sexting. We're all waiting."

"I'm not sexting. Not yet, anyway."

Shawn tensed, gripping the controller tightly and trying to keep his face carefully neutral.

"Oh yeah?" Jez, always interested in a bit of gossip, was immediately alert. "Who is it, then? A new flame?"

"An old one, actually. It's Sid—an ex from last year, although it was never serious. He moved away for a while, but he's back in Plymouth now. I think he's keen to start things up again."

The flash of jealousy that ripped through Shawn nearly took his breath away. He gritted his teeth.

"Do you still like him?" Jez asked. He put his controller down, clearly settling in to get the gory details.

Jude paused to type another message and then shrugged. "Yeah, I guess…. I mean, we were pretty compatible and he was a lot of fun. It ended because of him moving away, so now he's back, there's no reason not to pick things back up… given that I'm not involved with anyone."

Shawn knew the last part of that sentence was aimed directly at him.

"You should go for it, man," Mac said.

"Yeah, maybe." Jude looked at his phone again. "Actually, that sounds fun. That new club that opened recently—Troopers—is having an LGBT night tomorrow. Sid's going with a few other people and he's asking me if I want to come too."

"Cool," Jez said. "You should totally do it. God, I haven't been clubbing in ages."

"Why don't you come too?" Jude suggested. "I think I'm going to go. I haven't been out in a while, and I could use a bit of fun."

Was Shawn imagining the pressure of Jude's elbow against his ribs? Maybe it was just that the sofa was far too crowded.

"Yeah, that sounds awesome," Jez said enthusiastically. "What about you, Mac? You in? We could ask Dev and Ewan too, and maybe even see if we can get Josh and Rupert out—although they're like an old married couple these days, so they'll probably stay in and watch *Downton Abbey* or some shit like that."

"I'm game," Mac said.

Shawn sat in uncomfortable silence, his gut churning at the thought of Jude going out and meeting up with this Sid guy… kissing him and going home with him. Or fuck, maybe he'd even bring Sid back here.

Shawn suddenly realised he was at risk of cracking the game controller in his hand, so he hastily put it down on the coffee table—with more of a crash than he'd intended.

"Oh, sorry, Shawny." Jez leaned across Jude to pat him on the knee. "Are you feeling left out? You're welcome to come, of course, but I didn't think it would be your scene. If you're uncomfortable seeing me and Mac snogging on the sofa, you definitely don't want to see what happens on a dance floor at a gay club." He chuckled, obviously joking.

Shawn tried to muster up a laugh. That was how he would have responded a couple of weeks ago. "Yeah, probably not, mate." But his brain was emblazoned with fantasies about what sort of things *might* happen on the dance floor, and he was simultaneously aroused and wildly jealous at the thought of Jude dancing with Sid.

"Yeah. *Definitely* not Shawn's scene," Jude chimed in.

He sounded more wistful than bitter, but if Jez and Mac noticed the edge to his tone, they didn't comment on it.

Something twisted in Shawn's chest. He picked up his controller again. "Whatever. Are we playing this game or not?"

That signalled the end of the conversation and they went back to playing. But Shawn was too irritated to concentrate, and he kept missing the bends and falling off the track, which only made his mood worse.

He stuck it out for a couple more rounds, not wanting to look like he was desperate to escape, before making his excuses and heading back up his room so he could sulk in peace.

Shawn's shitty mood persisted all day Saturday despite his best efforts to pull himself out of it.

He went to the gym in the afternoon, then for a run afterwards. But even the treat of blue skies and autumn sunshine couldn't dispel the cloud of gloom in his head.

By the evening, he was back in sweatpants and sitting on the sofa in front of crappy TV, eating his feelings in the form of cold macaroni cheese out of a can and washing it down with cheap lager.

Jez breezed in. "Did I leave my phone in here? Oh yeah, there it is." He picked it up from the coffee table. When he straightened up, he rolled his eyes when he saw the state of Shawn. "Keeping it classy there, Shawny? Could you not even be bothered to put it in a bowl and heat it up?"

"Dev was using the microwave and I couldn't be arsed to wait. It tastes like shite whether it's hot or cold anyway. So…." He shrugged and poked the stuff with his fork.

"Yuck. Well, I'll leave you to it. I need to get ready to go out and party. Are you sure you don't wanna come to Troopers with us?" He sounded serious.

Shawn studied him, trying to decide on his motives. Was he taking the piss? "I don't think it's a good idea."

"There'll be friends and allies there too. It won't all be LGBT people, you know."

Shawn couldn't say that he claimed one of those letters for himself now. "I know," he said instead. "But I'm not really in the mood."

"Yeah. You've seemed a bit down this week. Anything you want to talk about?"

It was tempting. Jez was a good bloke, and Shawn trusted him. He took a breath, thinking about spilling his guts.

But then Dev came in with a plate of food, and Shawn had missed his chance.

"Nah, I'm good. But thanks." He gave Jez a quick smile. *Maybe another time.*

"Hey Dev, do you and Ewan fancy coming out tonight? We're going clubbing," Jez said.

"Oh yeah, Jude already asked us. But no thanks. Clubbing's not really my thing—way too loud and crowded." Dev winced at the mere mention of it. "Ewan and I are going to the cinema instead."

"No worries. Have a good night, then." Jez put his phone in his pocket and left.

Well, Shawn wouldn't have too much competition for the remote control tonight if everyone was out apart from him and Ben, who was bound to spend most of the evening in his room as usual. He sighed and scooped up another forkful of the bland, creamy, cheesy mush.

At least he had plenty of beer.

Shawn was still sitting on the sofa when Mac and Jude came in dressed for clubbing. After finishing his macaroni cheese, Shawn had polished off a bag of Doritos too. He had three empty cans of lager lined up in front of him and was partway down the fourth. The alcohol was dulling his senses but had done nothing to lift his spirits.

"*The X Factor?*" Mac raised his eyebrows. "Isn't there anything better on? Or do you fancy one of the contestants?"

Shawn shrugged. Sunk in his misery, he wasn't really paying much attention to the TV anyway. "Some of them are pretty easy on the eye."

Speaking of easy on the eye, Jude looked way too fucking hot for Shawn's liking. He was wearing tight black jeans, which showed off the curve of his arse and the length of his legs, and a red T-shirt with the words "SAVE A VIRGIN. DO ME INSTEAD" on the front in big white letters. Shawn was relieved to see he had a jacket slung over one arm. It probably wouldn't be the best idea for him to be walking around the city centre at night with that slogan showing.

Jude was talking on his phone. "Yeah, cool. Okay, mate. We'll find you there. See you in about half an hour." He ended the call. "Sid's in The Anchor with a few people. Is Jez nearly ready to go?"

"I think so." Mac flopped down on the sofa next to Shawn. "He was still pissing around with his hair a few minutes ago, but he won't be much longer."

Jude sat on the other sofa and ran a hand through his messy curls. Shawn's fingers itched to do the same. The shadow of stubble on his jaw was appealing too. Shawn wanted to touch that to remind himself how it felt—preferably with his lips.

Jude's phone chimed with a text and he looked at the screen with a smirk before typing something back.

Fucking Sid. Shawn wondered what they were saying to each other. The idea that Jude might hook up with Sid tonight burned like acid in his guts. He tried to stay focused on the TV and ignore the others, wishing they'd fuck off and leave him in peace, so he picked up the remote and flicked channels.

Casualty had just started on BBC1. That probably suited his mood better. Watching other people having shitty things happen to them might make his own life feel like less of a clusterfuck.

Finally, Jez turned up. "Okay, guys, I'm good to go. Sorry to keep you waiting, but it takes effort to look this pretty." He tossed his mess of dirty blond hair out of one eye. It looked as if he'd just crawled out of bed, but that was obviously the effect he was going for, and it suited him. "Come on."

He stood in front of Mac and offered a hand. Mac took it, and Jez hauled him up.

Mac put a possessive hand on the back of Jez's neck and kissed him lightly on the lips. "You look awesome, babe."

Jude stood too, putting his phone in his back pocket.

"Bye, mate," Mac said.

Jez waggled his fingers. "Yeah, bye, Shawny. Have a nice night."

Jude didn't say anything at all, but their gazes locked briefly as he followed the others out, closing the door behind him. Shawn thought he saw a flash of hurt on Jude's face. He took small comfort in the fact that he wasn't the only one feeling crap about where they'd ended up. He was sure Sid would be a good distraction, though.

With that thought he settled back on the sofa to watch other people's lives falling apart.

Shawn found *Casualty* weirdly absorbing. Not a show he usually watched, the story arcs involving the regular characters didn't mean much to him, but the story lines for this episode involved a car accident, a brawl in a pub, and a teenage girl who'd taken a drug overdose, and those held his attention. The car accident plot line was a little too close to home, given that the victim was a bloke who'd been on his way to tell a girl that he loved her after he'd been a twat.

Now it looked like he might end up dead before he got the chance to say his piece.

The living room door opened, making him jump. Lost in the drama on-screen, he'd forgotten he wasn't alone in the house.

"Oh. Hi." Ben stood uncertainly in the doorway, a bowl of food in his hands. "I thought you'd gone out with the others."

"No." Shawn picked up his beer and drained the can. He couldn't be bothered to move and get another. "You gonna join me? Although if you're squeamish, it might not be a good idea to watch this while you're eating." The scenes of the medics working on the car accident victims were pretty graphic. There was blood everywhere.

"Nah, I'm not squeamish." Ben came and sat on the sofa with Shawn and dug into his bowl of what looked like stir-fry.

It smelled good. About a million times better than the crap Shawn had eaten this evening. He realised that even though Ben had been living here a couple of months now, he had barely exchanged more than a few words with him. He didn't even know what Ben was studying, only that he was a mature student—in his mid-twenties, apparently—which was why he'd opted not to live in halls of residence. He didn't look any older than an undergrad, though. If Shawn didn't know better, he'd have assumed Ben was still a teenager.

He suddenly noticed he was watching Ben like a creeper, so he turned his attention back to the TV and gave a sigh that came out louder than he'd intended.

"You all right?" Ben eyed him doubtfully.

"Yeah," Shawn lied.

He was far from all right. He was a cowardly twat who was sitting here sulking and alone because he didn't have the balls to be honest about who he was.

Maybe it was the beer, or maybe Shawn was turning soft, but when the guy on *Casualty* pulled through after some emergency surgery and finally got to tell his girl that he loved her, Shawn had a massive lump in his throat. He swallowed hard, glad that Ben was watching the screen rather than him because he suspected his eyes would be a little misty.

"Love conquers all," Ben said, sounding a little cynical. "Shame it's not always that easy in real life."

"Yeah."

But maybe it could be.

The credits started to roll, and before he had time to think about what he was doing, Shawn was on his feet in a shower of Dorito crumbs.

"You off to bed?" Ben asked.

"No. I've decided to go out after all."

Out being the operative word. Shawn's stomach lurched with nerves, but his resolve held.

"Oh, okay. Well… have fun."

"Cheers." Shawn wasn't sure how much fun it would be, depending on the outcome, but anything would beat sitting around being helpless and pathetic. And with that thought in mind, he headed upstairs to get ready.

By the time he'd showered, fixed his hair, and tried on several different combinations of clothes until he was happy with his appearance, it was quarter to eleven. *Which pub was it they said they were going to?*

They might have already gone on to the club by now to beat the queues on the door.

Shawn didn't want to tell Jude he was coming. He wanted to surprise him, for better or worse. Instead he texted Jez before leaving the house.

Where are u?

At Troopers. Why?

Shawn didn't reply again. He hoped that exchange wouldn't be remarkable enough for Jez to mention it to anyone else. He put his phone in his pocket.

What the fuck am I doing?

He had no plan, no speech prepared—he was going to have to wing it. All he could hope was that he got there before Jude hooked up with Sid. So he put on his jacket, squared his shoulders, and set off into the night.

CHAPTER FIFTEEN

Jude stood at the edge of the dance floor, knocking back his pint. He'd stuck to shots in the pub because he didn't like being too full of beer when dancing, but now he was thirsty and the lager was refreshing. With the alcohol coursing through his veins and the thump of the bass vibrating in his bones, he felt exhilarated and ready to party.

Though still relatively early, the club had filled up fast. The doors had opened at ten, and the promise of low-priced drinks for the first hour had tempted people away from the pubs. A queue had been forming when they arrived at half past, and it took them a while to get in. At this rate the bouncers would be turning people away later.

Sid was already dancing, along with Jez and a few of the others they'd met in the pub.

Mac came back from the toilet, and put a hand on Jude's shoulder. "You coming to dance?"

"Yeah, in a minute." Jude lifted his pint. "Unless you want to help me with this?" There were no tables free. If he put his drink down, he'd probably never see it again.

Mac took it with a grin and downed most of what was left. "There. I'll buy you another one later."

Jude rolled his eyes. "Cheers."

When they approached the dance floor, a group parted to let them in. Jez immediately latched onto Mac, putting his arms around his neck and grinding on his thigh. They smiled at each other, gazes locked, and Jude felt a pang of envy for what they had together.

Just then, a hand on his shoulder reminded him that he could get laid tonight if that was what he wanted. Sid had been flirting with him by text earlier, and Jude had flirted back. Neither had made any promises, but Jude knew Sid was there for the taking.

Sid pulled him around and started to dance with him. His eyes were hot and interested. He ran his hands up Jude's stomach and chest, laughing as he read the words that had been hidden by Jude's jacket in the pub.

"Nice T-shirt." He grinned, then leaned in close so Jude could hear him clearly over the music. "And it makes sense. I wouldn't want to waste time on a virgin when I know what a good fuck you are."

Jude chuckled, gripping Sid's hips and tugging him closer. "You're not so bad yourself."

Maybe he should just go along with this. He and Sid had always been good together. It would be easy, familiar—and not in a bad way. Sid might help to erase the thoughts of Shawn that wouldn't leave his head.

He let Sid cup his jaw and guide him into a kiss. It was a good kiss, confident and full of promise.

But it jarred. Everything felt wrong. Longing for Shawn was like a spike twisting in his chest. He wasn't going to be able to fuck Shawn out of his system tonight, and he didn't think it was fair on Sid to try while he felt like this. He pulled away gently and shook his head.

"No?" Sid raised his eyebrows, regret written on his features.

"Sorry," Jude said. Then he spoke into Sid's ear. "It's nothing personal. But I'm hung up on someone else."

"Aw, baby. And he doesn't want you?"

Jude shrugged. "I think he does. But it's complicated."

"Well, it's his loss." Sid drew away and smiled.

Jude smiled back. Sid was a good guy.

They carried on dancing close together. Their bodies moved in sync and it was fun and flirty and a little bit sexy. But now they'd established it wasn't going anywhere, Jude was free to enjoy it without worrying he was leading Sid on.

Jude spotted a guy watching them over Sid's shoulder, his attention particularly focused on Sid's arse as he moved sinuously to the rhythm. The guy, who was wearing a white T-shirt that showed off his Mediterranean colouring, caught Jude's eye and raised his brows.

Jude spun Sid around so his back was pressed against Jude's front. "You've got an admirer," he said into Sid's ear.

Sid shivered at Jude's breath and ground his arse against Jude's dick, which was half-hard—he might have Shawn on the brain, but he was twenty years old and not made of stone. Sid turned his head and asked, "Where?"

"The hot dude with black hair and a white T-shirt." Jude beckoned to white-T guy, who was eye-fucking Sid blatantly now. The guy's eyes lit up and he approached like a panther stalking prey.

"Hi." He leaned in close to make himself heard. "You looking for a third?"

"We're not together," Sid said.

"Even better." White-T guy put his hands on Sid's hips and moved even closer. He glanced at Jude. "You mind if I join you?"

They danced like that for the next song. Sid looked in heaven sandwiched between them, and the whole thing was pretty fucking hot even though Jude wasn't in the mood to hook up. The chemistry between Sid and white-T guy, whose name was Leon, was off the charts, and it was impossible for Jude not to pick up on that. He drew back to adjust his boner, and that was when he realised he was being watched by someone else.

Someone familiar.

His heart skipped a beat.

Shawn stood on the edge of the dance floor, studying the three of them, his expression stricken. His gaze locked with Jude's and they stared at each other. Jude froze, a lone statue in the sea of moving bodies. He let his hands drop by his sides.

"What's the matter?" Leon asked, frowning.

"Huh?" Sid turned to see Jude's face. "What's up, Jude?"

Jude found his voice. "Uh… nothing. There's just someone I need to talk to. You guys have fun."

He broke away and left them to their dancing. Walking across the dance floor, his heart pounded faster than the bass and his palms sweated. He held Shawn's gaze. Shawn's face was tense, and for a moment he looked like he was going to turn and bolt. But he stood his ground. Jude's mind turned over with possibilities, trying to think of explanations for Shawn's presence here. He tried not to let his hopes rise too much.

"Hey," he said when he reached Shawn.

"Hey." Shawn's lips moved but Jude could barely hear him over the music.

He moved closer and put his lips near Shawn's ear. "What the hell are you doing here?" He caught the scent of Shawn's skin; it sent a powerful surge of longing through him.

"I don't know," Shawn replied. "It was stupid. You're obviously busy. I should go." Bitterness bled through his voice like acid. "I'm sorry to have interrupted your little threesome. And here I was thinking that Sid was my only competition."

With that, he drew back and turned away, heading towards the exit.

"No!" Jude ran after Shawn and grabbed his arm. Anger ripped through him at Shawn's dismissive words, but the hope was still there, burning brighter by the second. "Don't be an idiot. Fuck! It's too noisy in here for this. Come this way." He pulled Shawn through some double doors into a hallway. It was a little quieter there and less crowded, although a few groups of people hung around chatting and a couple were making out in the corner.

He squared up to Shawn again. "I was just dancing, for fuck's sake. I already told Sid I'm not interested in hooking up tonight. Anyway, what is it to you? If you came here to say something to me, fucking *say* it, Shawn!" His voice rose and a few people around them turned to listen.

They stared at each other. Shawn's brow furrowed and he set his jaw in determination. "Okay." He swallowed; his gaze flickered around nervously before settling back on Jude. "I came to tell you I want to go out with you. Date you. Be your boyfriend… lover, whatever you want to call it. And I'll tell people we're together. Maybe not everyone immediately… can you give me time to tell my family? But we don't have to keep it a secret from our friends."

Jude gaped at him. This was more than he could possibly have hoped for. He'd expected some sort of jealous outburst, maybe a plea to start something up again, but he'd never dared to hope that Shawn would be ready to make those kind of promises. "Are you sure?" he asked urgently. "What's changed since last week?"

Shawn shrugged. "I realised I was being an idiot and I don't want to lose the chance to be with you—if you still want me?" He waited, hope and uncertainty in his eyes.

Jude realised all the other conversations around them had ceased. Even the couple in the corner had stopped snogging and were watching them. Everyone was poised, waiting for him to answer.

"Yes," he said, and he could almost feel the collective sigh of relief around him. "Yes, of course I still want you, you twat."

Someone snorted with laughter.

Elation bubbled up, and a smile spread over his face to match the one dawning on Shawn's. "And it's fine for you to tell your family in your own time. That's not my business. I'm sorry if I made it sound like I needed you to be out to everyone. I don't. Just… you know. Our housemates would be a start."

"Yeah, we can definitely tell them."

They were still grinning at each other.

"Oh my God, are you ever going to fucking kiss each other, or what?" said a girl with purple hair. "Come on, guys, surely that's how this movie ends?"

A few chuckles greeted her words, plus a few whoops of encouragement and a shout of "Yeah, come on!"

They both moved at the same time, closing the gap until they met in an awkward mash of lips. Definitely not a kiss worthy of the big screen, but no less perfect for that. Jude felt Shawn's smile against his own, and then they finally managed to line their mouths up properly. The kiss got a little deeper and more serious, while the people surrounding them clapped and cheered.

Finally they pulled apart.

Shawn, flushed, looked sheepishly around at their audience. "Right, um, I think we'll leave you in peace."

"Congrats, guys." The purple-haired girl gave them a thumbs up. "That was beautiful."

Chatter started up around them again as Jude took Shawn's hand. "Where do you wanna go? Home?" The idea of getting Shawn into his bed again was very appealing.

Shawn shook his head. "No, not yet." He sounded determined. "I want to dance with you."

"Yeah?" That idea had possibilities too. "Jez and Mac are out there, remember. Are you ready for this?"

"Yes," Shawn said with no hesitation. "What better way to come out to them?" He leaned in close and said quietly, for Jude's ears only. "I want to go out there and show everyone that I'm yours."

Heat flashed through Jude. He licked his lips and squeezed Shawn's hand. "Fuck yes. Let's do it."

A wave of warmth and sound engulfed them as they went back through the doors to the dance floor. Shawn kept hold of Jude's hand as Jude led the way through the crowds. Mac was easy to spot, his head that little bit higher than most of the others. Jude moved towards him, a heady mixture of possessiveness and happiness swirling inside him.

They claimed a little space in the throng of dancing people. Jude started moving to the beat and tugged Shawn in close, his hands on his waist. Shawn was a decent dancer, not enough movement in his hips at first, but he loosened up quickly as Jude guided him, straddling one of Shawn's thighs and grinding up against him. Jude let his hands wander, stroking Shawn's chest and shoulders. Shawn brought his hands down to grab Jude's arse and tugged him closer still. Jude felt the hardness of Shawn's erection, then warm breath on his neck. That turned into soft lips moving in a ticklish trail up his jaw until at last their mouths locked in a passionate, lingering kiss.

Everything was heat and sweat and euphoria laced with the constant building pulse of arousal. Jude wondered how long it would take the others to notice who he was dancing with.

Mine, mine, mine—the word echoed through him with every beat of the music. The need to take Shawn home and show him all the other ways he belonged to Jude was growing every minute.

Jude broke away from the kiss reluctantly and put a little space between them, his hands still around Shawn's neck. Shawn's pupils were huge, lips wet in the flashing club lights. He blinked, looking dazed, and reached down to adjust his dick before putting his hands back on Jude's hips.

Jude had the same problem himself; if they hadn't stopped when they did, he'd be getting into blue-balls territory. He glanced around to see where their mates were.

Sid and Leon danced wrapped around each other. *Awesome*. He didn't need to feel guilty for blowing Sid off now that it looked like he was in for a good night. Jez and Mac were a little farther away, also lost in each other and oblivious to anyone else.

Fuck's sake. It was typical that Jez, who was normally very observant and way too damn nosey, would be failing to pay attention when Jude actually *wanted* him to see something.

Just then, Mac lifted his head from where he'd been sucking on Jez's neck, and he caught sight of Jude. His gaze flickered from Jude to Shawn. His brow drew down and his eyes narrowed. He glanced at Jude again, then back to Shawn, as if he couldn't believe what his eyes were showing him.

Jude grinned and waved, at which point Shawn turned his head so Mac could see him face-on.

"Fuck!" Mac gaped.

Jude didn't need any lip-reading skills to interpret that reaction.

Jez turned around to see what the fuss was about and his jaw dropped in cartoon slow motion.

Shawn laughed. "I think we just blew Jez's mind."

"I dunno. Let's make sure." Jude tugged him closer again, just so they wouldn't be in any doubt at all about what was going on here. He took Shawn's face in his hands and pulled him in for another kiss.

"What the fuck, guys?" A punch in the arm and Jez's voice interrupted their PDA. Jez gestured between them. "Seriously. What is this? It's November, so it can't be April Fool's. So what? How is this happening? Shawn's straight!"

"Not so much, it turns out." Jude had to shout over the music. This really wasn't the ideal place for an in-depth analysis of the hows and whys.

Shawn obviously felt the same. "I'll tell you about it tomorrow," he promised.

"You'd better!" Jez still looked as if he thought this was some sort of prank.

Mac smiled at them. "Good on you." He offered his fist to Shawn to bump, and then to Jude. Then he said something to Jez that Jude didn't catch and guided Jez back to dance again.

"Do you wanna dance more?" Jude asked Shawn.

Shawn shook his head. "No. Take me home." Then, with his lips right up by Jude's ear, he added, "And fuck me."

CHAPTER SIXTEEN

The walk home was sweet torture for Shawn.

Being with Jude was awesome, and Shawn held his hand once they got away from the city centre and onto the quieter residential streets. But the knowledge of what was coming made him painfully excited, and walking with the boner to end all boners wasn't comfortable given the snugness of his jeans.

Jude wasn't helping matters by insisting on using the walk to plan what they were going to do. He squeezed Shawn's hand and leaned in close as he asked in a low voice, "Do you want me to tie you up?"

"I don't know." Shawn shivered with anticipation. "I don't think so. Not this time."

"But you want me to top you? Boss you around?"

"Yes. Fuck." Shawn adjusted himself yet again. His dick was sticking out of the top of his underwear and rubbing on the waistband of his jeans in a not-fun way. He shoved it to a better angle.

"Stop groping yourself in public. You'll get us arrested." Jude's voice was warm with amusement.

"Stop talking dirty, then. You're driving me crazy."

"Poor baby. Not long to wait now."

They had just rounded the corner into their street, and Shawn breathed a sigh of relief. *Nearly home.*

When they reached the doorstep, Jude was the first to get his keys out. He unlocked the door and Shawn followed him inside.

"Straight upstairs?" Jude asked.

"Yeah."

Nerves fluttered in Shawn's belly as he followed Jude up the two flights to his room at the top. Shawn wished he could turn his thinking brain off, because it was messing with him. He wanted this, wanted Jude, but he was terrified too. Much as he'd loved having Jude's fingers in him the other night, Jude's cock was way bigger. What if he couldn't take it? What if he tried but hated being fucked? What if Jude was disappointed in him?

Jude led them into his room, turned the light on, then locked the door behind them. His bed was a mess of books and papers, so he quickly piled those up and moved them to his desk. Then he put the lamp on and turned the main light off.

"There, that's a bit more romantic. Although I guess I could have fucked you over the desk instead. It was tidier than the bed." He grinned.

Shawn gave a nervous laugh.

"Hey." Jude came up and put his hands on Shawn's face, holding him so that he had to meet Jude's gaze. "Are you freaking out?"

"Maybe a little." Shawn felt his cheeks heat.

Jude kissed his lips softly. "What do you need?"

Shawn took a shaky breath. "For you to take charge," he admitted.

It was hard to say what he wanted, but he needed this. He needed Jude to understand. "I want this, but I want you to tell me what to do. Use me how you want. I know you'll make it good for me too… I just…." His last words tumbled out in a rush. "I don't want to have to decide things."

"We can do that. As long as you promise me one thing. That if you don't like something or you want to stop, you'll tell me."

Shawn nodded. "Yeah, of course."

"And if it's easier, use the colour words. Yellow to slow down, red to stop, remember?"

"Yes."

"Promise." Jude's voice was utterly serious.

The subtle command in his tone made Shawn's body respond; a thrill ran through him. He straightened his shoulders. "I promise."

"Okay. Well, start by getting undressed. I want you naked. Put your clothes on the chair."

Obediently, Shawn stripped—jacket first, then shoes, T-shirt, jeans, and finally his socks and boxers. Jude watched him intently, making no move to follow suit. Shawn's skin prickled with the awareness of Jude's scrutiny and his already-hard cock got even harder, bobbing as he straightened up after taking off his underwear.

Jude's gaze raked over Shawn, taking in his chest and stomach, then settling on his dick. He licked his lips. "Fuck, you're gorgeous." He lifted a finger and spun it in a circle. "Turn around."

Cheeks burning and cock aching, Shawn turned. He swallowed, every nerve ending alight with expectation as he heard Jude move closer. Warm breath caressed Shawn's neck and the space between them became charged with electricity. Then one of Jude's hands skimmed over the curve of his arse. Fingers dipped into his crack and Shawn shivered, legs going weak. He felt needy, desperate. He wanted to bend over the desk and spread himself open, beg for Jude to touch him more.

Jude slipped his other hand around Shawn's cock and stroked him a few times. The touch was so good. Jude's fingers rubbed lightly over Shawn's hole and he gasped, pinned between the two sources of pleasure.

"Yeah," Jude murmured. "So good. I love how into this you are."

He carried on, pressing kisses to Shawn's neck and shoulder, and the world slipped away. All that mattered was Jude and the sweet sensation of his touch. Shawn's orgasm was building already, but he knew Jude wouldn't let him come yet, and that didn't even matter. This was all about the journey. Jude was in charge and that knowledge made him feel safe.

Sure enough, Jude stopped before Shawn got too close. "Not yet," he said. He guided Shawn around to face him and kissed him slow and deep. Then he drew back. "Kneel down. I want you to suck me."

Embarrassingly eager, Shawn dropped to his knees and immediately regretted his alacrity. The floorboards were hard.

Jude must have noticed the wince, because he got a pillow from the bed and put it down for him. "Kneel on that."

"Thanks." Shawn made himself comfortable and then looked up the length of Jude's body to his face.

"God, you look perfect like that." Jude put his hand under Shawn's chin and ran the pad of his thumb over his lips. "Come on, then. Get my cock out."

Shawn's fingers were sweaty and he fumbled with Jude's belt and fly. Once he got them open, he tugged Jude's trousers down a little and they fell the rest of the way to his knees. Jude was gratifyingly hard and straining against his underwear. Shawn pressed his face against the bulge for a moment, inhaling the heady masculine scent of him. Then he pulled Jude's boxers down so that his cock sprang free, dark and flushed and wet at the tip. The scent of musk was even stronger then, and it made Shawn's mouth water.

"Suck me," Jude said huskily.

The want in his voice ramped up Shawn's desire, but the urge to please Jude was greater than his own need for release. He used his hand to guide Jude's cock into his mouth.

It was easy in this position, easier than it had been last time with him on his back. He took Jude in deep and then drew back to suck on the head. He watched Jude's reactions, loving the way his eyes took on a glazed expression and his mouth grew slack.

"Fuck, yes." Jude stroked Shawn's hair, threading his fingers into the short strands, pulling him closer so he took Jude deeper again. "So fucking good."

Shawn gave in to it, letting his hands drop as Jude fucked his mouth in slow, careful strokes. His soft murmurs of approval and grunts of pleasure showed how much he was enjoying it. Shawn closed his eyes, the sight of Jude almost too much. He reached for his own cock and curled his fingers around it, starting to stroke.

"No!" Shawn snapped his eyes open to see Jude looking down at him. "Don't touch yourself. I want to be the one to make you feel good. You have to wait."

Shawn groaned, a flare of frustration and irritation making him want to challenge Jude on that, but he couldn't argue with Jude's dick in his mouth.

Jude had stopped moving and was just holding him steady as he stared him down. Jude seemed to guess Shawn's feelings on the matter, because he grinned. "You look even hotter when you're pissed off with me. You wanted this, remember? Unless you want to stop?" He watched Shawn carefully for a reaction.

In this position, Shawn couldn't use words, but he shook his head minutely. *No.*

"You okay to carry on?"

A tiny nod and a stroke of his tongue. *Yes.*

As Jude started to move again, Shawn sank deeper into a place where he didn't mind waiting. The sharp edge of his arousal, the building need was bearable because he knew that Jude would take care of him eventually and it would be worth waiting for. In the meantime that was enough.

More than enough.

He lost track of time, and when Jude finally eased his cock from his mouth, it could have been five minutes later or twenty. His jaw ached and he swallowed, tasting Jude's precome on his tongue.

Jude drew him up to stand and kissed him. Their erections bumped and Shawn pressed into the contact, desperate for Jude's touch.

"You were so good for me," Jude said when he broke the kiss. "Such a good little cocksucker."

His words sent a jolt of heat to Shawn's dick. It throbbed and ached. "Please," he begged, "fuck me."

"Soon. Get on the bed for me."

Shawn scrambled to comply, lying down on his back.

"No, on your hands and knees."

He turned over, kneeling and facing the headboard. Jude went to the drawer by the bed and rummaged around to get something, and then walked to the foot of the bed where Shawn could no longer see him. He heard the clink of Jude's belt buckle and the rustle of clothing. He looked over his shoulder to see Jude naked, a hand holding his cock as he stared at Shawn like he was the best thing he had ever seen.

"Shawn,"—Jude's voice was tight and breathless—"*God.*"

He didn't seem capable of elaborating, but Shawn assumed it was all good. He let his head drop, breathing hard and waiting for whatever Jude was going to give him.

Waiting till Jude was ready.

After what felt like forever, the mattress dipped as Jude joined him on the bed. Warm hands slid over Shawn's hips and back, and Jude's cock poked Shawn's balls. Jude covered Shawn's body with his own and pressed kisses up his spine, across his shoulders, and back down until his breath was hot in the crack of Shawn's arse. "Is this okay?" he asked.

"Yes." The word came out embarrassingly breathy and high-pitched.

And then Jude gripped Shawn's arse and opened him up. Shawn had a moment of self-consciousness—*Thank fuck I showered earlier*—but then Jude's mouth was on him and all coherent thoughts were driven from his brain. The touch of Jude's tongue as he licked over Shawn's hole was almost too much, yet not enough at the same time. The warm, wet tickle of it drove Shawn crazy, but had him begging for more, the words torn out of him almost without him choosing to say them. "Fuck, Jude. *Fuck*. I need more…. *Please*." His cock jerked beneath him in empty space, desperate for touch.

Jude's chuckle was muffled as he carried on, making Shawn curse again and curl his fingers into the sheets.

Finally, Jude stopped. As he drew back, the air was cool on Shawn's wet arse.

Shawn waited, exposed and vulnerable. He existed for Jude. Nothing else mattered in that moment. He'd take what Jude would give him, and he'd be grateful.

"You look amazing," Jude said softly. "So hot, waiting for me to fuck you."

Shawn made a small desperate sound. Words had become too hard to form.

He heard movement and the tear of a condom wrapper, followed shortly after by the click of a bottle cap. He waited, trying to calm his breathing. His heart was a frantic beat, keyed up with anticipation and a resurgence of nerves.

But instead of the nudge of Jude's cock that he was expecting, fingers pressed at his hole; the tip of one slid in easily and Jude pushed in a second alongside it.

"Come on, baby. Let me in." His voice was husky and soothing. It made Shawn want to be good for him. "That's it. Breathe."

Shawn hadn't even noticed that he'd stopped. He let his breath out slowly and with it, his body relaxed. Jude took advantage of that and pressed his fingers home in a careful slide. Shawn gasped as Jude found his prostate and rubbed it, easing in and out in small motions as Shawn's body adjusted more. Gradually Jude changed to longer, more insistent thrusts. Shawn moaned, rocking back to meet the movements. He wondered if he could come just from this, and what a prostate orgasm would feel like if he could. Maybe he'd get to find out.

"Is that good?"

Jude's self-control was impressive—he'd been hard since they started this.

"Yeah," Shawn managed. He wanted to ask for Jude's cock, but he couldn't concentrate on anything apart from the perfect, stretching slide of Jude's fingers stroking him higher and higher. His own fingers itched to reach for his erection, but one touch might be enough to tip him over the edge.

"I can't wait to get my cock inside you," Jude said, his control finally slipping. "Fuck, Shawn. You're so tight and hot inside. It's gonna feel so good."

"*Yes*," Shawn panted. "Need you… please… fuck me!"

Jude slipped his fingers free, leaving Shawn clenching on nothing, but he soon replaced them with the blunt head of his cock. "Here you go. Gonna give it to you." He pressed, and then groaned as he slid a little way inside.

Shawn tensed at the burning stretch. It felt like so much more than Jude's fingers, but when he realised Jude had paused and was waiting, he slowly relaxed again. Breathing deeply, he let his head drop. Looking down he saw his poor neglected cock, flushed and leaking precome; he was still hard, despite the discomfort. He took a few more breaths, and gradually the edge of pain dissipated and he could focus on the good feeling of fullness.

"Okay, give me more," he said.

Jude's fingers tightened on his hips, holding him steady as he pushed in slowly until he was all the way in, his body warm against Shawn's, his cock buried deep. "Okay?"

"Yeah," Shawn managed.

Oh, that hurt again. But not for long. As Jude rocked in with the tiniest, most cautious of movements, Shawn adjusted. Soon there was no discomfort, only building pleasure and the need for more. "That's good."

Good didn't really cover it. It was fucking amazing. Fireworks and shooting stars, and holy shit! Why hadn't he been fucking himself with a dildo ever since he worked out what masturbation was? Because *fuck*. Shawn's prostate was now the new centre of his universe.

"You ready for more?" Jude asked.

"Yes."

All conscious thought ceased as Jude started to fuck him harder. He went slow and steady at first, with long strokes that stole Shawn's breath and made him moan and curse, unintelligible words falling from his lips along with *yes* and *more*. Jude sped up, his hips snapping against Shawn's arse. Wonderful filthy sounds filled the room: skin on skin, harsh breathing and grunts and the creaking of the bed.

Shawn was driven to the brink, a mountain peak where he teetered on the edge of perfect desperation. "Need to come." It came out as a sob.

Jude stopped, and Shawn cried out in frustration as Jude started to pull out. "No, don't stop!"

"Shhh, it's okay." Jude patted his hip. "Roll over. I want to see you, and it will be easier for me to reach your cock this way."

Shawn hurriedly complied, sprawling out on his back and spreading his legs.

Jude pushed Shawn's knees back. "Hold yourself there." He lined his cock up again.

They both groaned as he slid home.

Jude grinned down at him, flushed and breathless. "Such a cockslut." But the way he said it didn't sound teasing. His voice was admiring, almost, and weirdly tender.

Shawn huffed out a laugh. "Yeah. Yeah, I guess I am."

Jude leaned down and kissed him as he started to thrust again. Shawn kissed him back greedily, trying to grind his dick against Jude's belly for some much-needed friction. But it still wasn't enough, and he whimpered in frustration.

"It's okay. I've got you." Jude broke the kiss, and the loss of his lips was balanced by the touch of his hand on Shawn's cock. He wrapped his hand around it loosely at first, thumbing over the head.

"Fucking tease," Shawn growled.

"Yeah, but you like it. You like being made to wait."

Shawn couldn't deny it, but he glared at Jude furiously as he fucked him in slow, leisurely strokes while he smeared Shawn's precome around and failed to jerk him off properly. In a fit of frustration, Shawn squeezed his muscles around Jude as he thrust in deep.

"Oh fuck." Jude's eyes flew wide open. "That feels amazing."

Shawn relaxed on the next thrust in before squeezing again. Jude responded by fucking him harder, groaning each time he bottomed out. Finally, Jude's control was slipping, and Shawn was the one making it happen.

At long last, Jude gripped Shawn's cock tightly, stroking him with perfect movements clearly designed to get him off. Tension built, a rising tide of surging pleasure ready to break.

About fucking time.

Their gazes locked. Jude was flushed and desperate, and Shawn imagined he must look the same. "Come on, baby," Jude muttered. "Come on."

And Shawn's orgasm crashed over him, devastating and blinding. He was dimly aware of crying out loudly as his whole body went taut, muscles contracting as he spilled in Jude's hand, slicking his grip.

"Oh fuck, *yes*," Jude groaned, fucking Shawn through it, thrusting in harder and faster, grinding into Shawn until his face contorted and he came too, cock pulsing as Shawn squeezed around him one last time.

As their breathing slowed, Jude gave Shawn the goofiest grin he had ever seen. "You okay there?"

Shawn blinked up at him, dazed. "I think so." He grinned back.

Still joined, Jude leaned down to kiss him again. This kiss was sweet and slow, nothing like the desperation of before. It made warm happiness spread in Shawn's chest, a yearning tug of hope. He bit back the urge to make crazy declarations. It was too soon to use words like *love*... but it definitely felt like love could be on the cards for them soon. He hoped Jude felt the same.

They separated when Jude's dick started to slip free, but only for long enough for Jude to deal with the condom and chuck it in the bin. He came straight back to snuggle under the covers.

"So, just to be clear... are we boyfriends now?" Jude asked. "Like an actual relationship, exclusive and stuff?"

"I hope so." Shawn felt a sudden lurch of anxiety. What if they weren't on the same page? Their conversation in the club earlier had been pretty rushed. "That's what I want."

Jude's smile was reassuring. "Good. Me too. I just wanted to be sure. I know this is all new for you."

Shawn didn't care about that any more. Here, in Jude's bed, everything seemed simple. The rest of the world could just deal with it. "Whatever. I've made up my mind."

"Awesome." Jude snuggled closer so they were nearly nose-to-nose in the warm cocoon of duvet. "I'm really happy we worked things out."

"Me too." Shawn pulled Jude into his arms and kissed him again.

Really fucking happy.

CHAPTER SEVENTEEN

The first thing Jude was aware of the next morning was warm arms around him.

Shawn.

Jude smiled before he even opened his eyes.

The next thing he noticed was Shawn's lips on his shoulder in a soft, sleepy kiss. Perhaps that was what had woken him. Jude hummed, snuggling back and putting his hand over Shawn's where it lay wrapped around his stomach. "Good morning."

This was so different from the other time Shawn had slept in his bed, when he'd bolted like a frightened rabbit the morning after.

"Morning." Shawn's voice was warm and raspy, like his chin where it brushed against Jude's skin.

"You're still here, then?" Jude said lightly.

Shawn froze. "Um...."

"That's a good thing, idiot." Jude rolled over to face him, grinning at Shawn's scowl. "I was teasing."

"Well, don't. It's too early for teasing."

"What time is it, anyway?"

"I dunno." Shawn put his hand on Jude's hip.

"Well, how do you know it's too early, then?" Jude stroked Shawn's chest, loving the feel of his smooth, warm skin. He smelled good too.

"Ugh. Whatever."

Jude slipped his hand lower, questing over Shawn's abs to find his cock and squeeze it. "Is it too early for this?"

Shawn chuckled. "It's never too early for that."

Shawn was soft, but he started to stiffen as soon as Jude touched him, thickening and filling his fist as he stroked. Jude moved in to kiss him, not caring about morning breath, because he needed to feel Shawn's lips.

Shawn didn't seem to mind. He reached for Jude, too, and they brought each other off like that between breathless kisses and smiles and moans of encouragement. Jude came first, with Shawn following soon after. When they were both done, they kissed a little more before separating for a half-hearted clean-up. The sheets were a lost cause, but they'd got pretty sticky last night anyway. Jude planned on messing them up again tonight, so really, there was no point in worrying about it. Jizz stains never killed anyone.

After that, they dozed again for a while.

Jude slipped in and out of sleep, warm and sated and ridiculously happy until finally his stomach started to rumble.

He nudged Shawn, who was lying on his back, snoring softly. "I'm hungry. I need to get up and get some breakfast. You wanna come? Or do you want to sleep more?"

Shawn grunted and opened his eyes blearily. He patted his belly. "Yeah... food sounds good."

They got up. Jude pulled on sweats and a T-shirt, but Shawn only had his clothes from the night before. "Wanna borrow some sweatpants?" he asked as Shawn picked up his jeans.

"Yeah, thanks."

Jude chucked him a pair of old grey ones that were pretty baggy on him, so they should be fine on Shawn. Shawn pulled them on commando, and Jude's attention shot to the outline of his dick. "Well, that's distracting."

Shawn grinned and shimmied his hips so his cock jiggled. "You sure you want breakfast? I've got something else you can put in your mouth."

"Dude, tasty though your dick is, I need more protein than you can provide. Maybe later."

As they descended the stairs, they heard voices coming from the kitchen, the deep boom of Mac's voice followed by laughter that was unmistakably Jez's.

"You ready for this?" Jude asked.

"Yeah." Shawn took his hand. "Totally."

When they walked through the door, the kitchen was crowded. As well as Jez and Mac, Dev and Ewan were there too, and even Ben. A full house.

"Good morning." Shawn's voice was carefully casual, but his hand, tight around Jude's, betrayed his tension.

The others turned and there was a short silence as they took in the sight of Jude and Shawn, hand in hand.

Jez broke the silence, grinning at them. "Good night, then, lads?"

Ewan smirked. "It certainly sounded like one."

Shawn made a choking noise and covered it with a cough.

"Oh. Were you sleeping here last night, then?" Jude asked. In the heat of the moment, he hadn't even considered that. Dev and Ewan split their time between Dev's room and Ewan's in the house next door. It was typical that they were there last night when he and Shawn had been particularly loud. Good thing they weren't trying to keep this a secret.

"Well, sleeping is a bit of a stretch given the racket you two were making. But yes."

"Can I die now, please?" Shawn muttered.

Jude squeezed his hand. "You said you were ready to be out and proud. No shame, babe. It's not like we haven't heard the rest of them enough times."

"So." Jez folded his arms. "Now we've established that I wasn't hallucinating last night and you two really were making out on the dance floor and fucking like bunnies when you got home, can you put me out of my misery and explain how the hell this happened?"

Everyone looked expectantly at Shawn, including Jude.

"Well—" Shawn cleared his throat. "—I... uh, I'm bi. I think. It just took me a while to admit it to myself and actually do something about it."

"No shit." Jez raised his eyebrows.

"I told you he was in denial!" Ewan burst out gleefully. "I fucking *told* you and none of you believed me."

"I did!" Jude protested.

"Seriously?" Shawn rounded on him. "When did you wankers have this discussion about me? And how long have you been talking about me behind my back?"

Jude flushed and said a little sheepishly, "It was no big deal. Just something that came up one time when you were a twat about Dev and Ewan kissing."

Shawn looked stricken and Jude felt bad for reminding him about that night. He'd already apologised for it.

"Oh yeah," Shawn muttered, "I remember. Fuck, I was an arsehole. I'm sorry."

"Yeah, you were," Ewan said, but then he smiled. "But I think we can let you off. You've come a long way since then."

Shawn held up his and Jude's joined hands. "Yeah." He turned to Jude and tugged him closer. He pressed a chaste kiss on his cheek that made Jude's heart do a little flip, and then Shawn put his arm around him and beamed. "I guess I have."

EPILOGUE

A few weeks later

Shawn sat in the chair in his room, shirtless, his sweatpants pushed down around his hips, his laptop open on the desk in front of him. He stroked himself slowly, riding the delicious crest of arousal as he watched Jude on the screen. A quick glance at the clock told him that there wasn't long to wait now. Jude's show was nearly over; he'd be going for the grand finale any minute now.

Jude chuckled in response to a comment. "Thanks, I'm glad you approve of my cock. I'm pretty fond of it myself."

His boyfriend likes it too.

Shawn felt a familiar flash of jealousy when he remembered other people got to see Jude like this.

They'd discussed how to handle Jude's cam shows when they made things official between them. Jude hadn't wanted to stop, because he needed the money, and Shawn didn't really have a problem with it. The thing they *had* both agreed on, though, was that Jude would go back to doing them solo. Neither of them wanted to play out their relationship on camera any more. It was private now, for them alone. So they got around Shawn feeling weird about Jude's shows by including him in a way only they knew about. Jude knew Shawn was watching and waiting for him to finish.

Shawn smiled as he watched Jude stroke himself faster, getting flushed and breathless.

He's mine. I'm the only one who gets to touch him. I'm the only one who gets fucked by him.

Shawn was getting close now, so he stopped stroking, teasing the head with his thumb as he watched Jude's hand speed up on his cock.

"Oh yeah," Jude gasped out. "Yeah, fuck. I'm nearly there."

The urge to come with him was hard to resist, but Shawn was practised at this now. Jude would make it worth his while if he held off.

Jude arched and came with a cry, the sound tinny on Shawn's laptop, a shadow of the real thing. Shawn tensed, his cock flexing in his hand as he bit his lip so hard it hurt.

Hurry up.

Jude rushed through his usual goodbye spiel and cut the camera feed.

Shawn counted slowly in his head as he waited, hand gripping his cock, stroking just enough to keep him close, ready for Jude. He heard footsteps on the stairs, then a *tap-tap-tap* on his door. He stood, pulled up his sweatpants, and hurried to open the door.

Jude stood there, hair tousled as if he'd pulled on his T-shirt in a hurry, pyjama bottoms low on his hips.

"Finally," Shawn said.

"Hey, baby." Jude raked his gaze down Shawn's torso to the tent in his sweats. "Have you been a good boy?"

"Aren't I always?" Shawn grabbed his arm and tugged Jude inside so he could close and lock the door behind him. Shawn prided himself on his ability to wait.

"Yeah, you are." The approval in Jude's tone made Shawn flush with pride and the desire to please him even more. "Now get naked and get back in that chair."

Shawn hurried to comply, shedding his clothes in a heap on the floor and turning his desk chair to be face-to-face with Jude. He sat down and spread his legs, his cock poking up eagerly. He let his hands drop by his sides, knowing not to touch himself now Jude was here.

Jude stood and looked at him for a moment, arms folded and a dirty grin on his face. His gaze made Shawn's skin prickle; the awareness of being studied so closely raised goosebumps on his skin. Even though it was untouched, his cock got even harder, balls aching with the need for release.

"You look so fucking hot like that," Jude said in a low, smoky voice. "Sitting there, waiting for me so patiently." He stepped closer, dropped to his knees between Shawn's legs, still not touching him, and looked up at Shawn through his lashes. "Did you enjoy watching me tonight?"

"Yeah," Shawn managed, his voice strained.

"I love knowing you're watching my shows." Jude put his hands on Shawn's knees and slid them slowly up his thighs. "Knowing you're watching and touching yourself makes me so fucking hot." He licked his lips. "But knowing you're waiting for me to make you come afterwards is the best thing of all."

Shawn took a shaky breath, clenching his fists to stop himself from grabbing Jude's head and guiding him to where he wanted him. Where he needed him.

"Are you ready to come now?" Jude's warm breath skimmed the head of Shawn's cock and it jerked. A pearl of precome leaked from his slit and slid down the shaft.

"Fuck, yes. *Please.*" Shawn knew Jude liked it when he begged. It usually got Shawn what he wanted.

Sure enough, he was rewarded. He groaned as Jude took him into the perfect wet heat of his mouth and sucked him deep. Jude seemed to be done with teasing, because he set a pace that meant it wasn't going to take long. Shawn watched his cock disappearing between the stretch of Jude's lips. Jude looked up and sucked harder.

"Gonna come," Shawn gasped.

Jude made a sound of encouragement, and that was all it took. Shawn thrust into Jude's mouth, hips lifting without his conscious permission, and only then did he allow himself to put his hands on Jude's head, tangling his fingers in Jude's dark curls as he came hard, his orgasm stretching out in a series of dizzying pulses until he almost couldn't take any more.

"Fuck," he said weakly. He loosened his grip on Jude's hair as Jude pulled off, grinning and breathless. "That was fucking intense. I thought my balls were gonna explode tonight."

"Pretty sure they just did." Jude licked his lips. "In my mouth."

Shawn chuckled.

Jude got to his feet and offered Shawn a hand up from the chair. Shawn took it gratefully, his legs still wobbly from coming so hard. Luckily he only needed to make it far as the bed for the post-orgasm cuddling. Jude stripped naked before joining Shawn and pulling the covers over them both.

Shawn sighed happily. "That was so hot. Watching you drives me crazy in the best way. It reminds me how I felt that first time...."

"When you stalked me online like a creeper and I blew your tiny mind?" Jude supplied.

"Fuck you!" Shawn dug him in the ribs and tickled until he squirmed away protesting. "Okay sorry, sorry!"

"But yes," Shawn said a little sheepishly. "That time."

Jude rolled on top of him and grabbed his wrists, pinning them. "I'm glad you stalked me like a creeper. Otherwise we wouldn't be here now."

"True."

They grinned at each other, and Shawn's heart swelled with affection and the sense of rightness he always felt when he was with Jude. "I love you."

It wasn't the first time he'd said those three little words to Jude, but it still felt like a novelty.

Jude dipped his head for a kiss, keeping Shawn waiting—as usual. Eventually he broke away and murmured, "I love you too."

Shawn would never get tired of hearing it.

About the Author

Jay lives just outside Bristol in the West of England. He comes from a family of writers, but always used to believe that the gene for fiction writing had passed him by. He spent years only ever writing emails, articles, or website content.
One day, Jay decided to try and write a short story—just to see if he could—and found it rather addictive. He hasn't stopped writing since.

Jay is transgender and was formerly known as she/her.

Connect with Jay
www.jaynorthcote.com
Twitter: @Jay_Northcote
Facebook: Jay Northcote Fiction

More from Jay Northcote

Novels and Novellas
Cold Feet
Nothing Serious
Nothing Special
Nothing Ventured
Not Just Friends
Passing Through
The Little Things
The Dating Game – Owen & Nathan #1
The Marrying Kind – Owen & Nathan #2
Helping Hand – Housemates #1
Like a Lover – Housemates #2
Practice Makes Perfect – Housemates #3
What Happens at Christmas
The Law of Attraction
Imperfect Harmony
Into You
A Family for Christmas

Short Stories (ebook only)
Top Me Maybe?
All Man

Free Reads (ebook only)
Coming Home
First Class Package
Why Love Matters

Jay also has several titles available in audiobook via Audible, Amazon or Apple.

Made in the USA
Charleston, SC
23 January 2017